# DEATH CALLERS

RAVEN HUDGINS

*I want to dedicate this book to my late grandfather Gene Krigsvold and his brother—my late great-uncle—Gary Krigsvold.*

# Acknowledgements

I want to thank all my friends and family for their support—y'all know who you are.

# Chapter 1

My mother had always told me that when I turned eighteen and had my first Death Call it would change my life. I just didn't know how right she would be. "I, Aislin Briella Gray, am a banshee, and I see death."

****

"Happy Birthday, Aislin!"

I turned just in time to see Kaydynce bounding toward me. Her short blond hair danced as she ran. Her body barreled into me with the force of a wrecking ball. I barely caught myself before her arms encircled my waist. She lifted me off the ground and twirled me like a rag doll.

"Thanks, Kay," I breathed, trying to fill my lungs once more.

My fingers fumbled with the combination lock on my locker. The damn thing shifted and blurred in my vision. In my peripheral, Kaydynce's lips curved upward. Her sapphire eyes twinkled in the fluorescent lighting.

"I can't believe you're eighteen now! You are so lucky," she sighed and leaned against the locker beside mine, one hand pressed against her forehead, head thrown back, like the women in black and white movies. I rolled my eyes at her antics. "I can't wait to turn eighteen so I can do Death Calls with y'all!" Her tinkling voice carried through the hall.

Movement behind Kaydynce caught my eye. Red-brown hair reflected in the lighting, offset by a lean build. My heart skipped a beat. Could it be? Instinctively my body inched away from the cold metal.

"You know nothing, Kaydynce, and never will..." my other friend, Teagan, hissed.

Her tone snapped me back to reality. I glanced at her then again to the crowded hallway, but he was gone. I focused back onto her face. Her green eyes were glassed over, sucked into her own world. I had seen that expression before, in my mother's eyes. Some would say 'dead' eyes. Chills ran down my arms at the mere word.

Teagan was the oldest of my little banshee group while Kaydynce was the youngest. Both Kaydynce and I studied Teagan, our brows scrunched. I had never heard so much resentment in her voice before. Kaydynce shrugged and turned toward me, blocking out Teagan's silhouette.

"Don't listen to her, Aislin," she said, waving her hand in the air. "You should be overjoyed that you finally get to be a true banshee!"

"Shhh, not so loud."

She brushed it off, putting her arm around my waist and dragged me toward first period. I scanned the sea of students to make sure we hadn't been overheard or at least that's what I told myself. My eyes searched for the guy who had made my heart skip and beat on overtime. I took a deep breath and tried to calm the gut feeling that something bad was about to happen. Teagan shook her head, her black curls swaying and followed close behind.

My thoughts carried me forward. What happened? Who was this person? She wasn't always like this...was she? No. I shook my head. It wasn't like her. She used to be the fun one, until her eighteenth birthday a few months ago, and then everything changed. I wasn't sure what had happened that night, but I knew it had been horrible. She never talked about it, though. Was I a bad friend?

I had a sickening feeling that the same thing was going to happen to me. I tried to think positive as we shuffled into our first period class, Chemistry.

Kaydynce, Teagan, and I sat in the back of the room. A safe place to hide from prying eyes and yet even sitting in the back we got glances and stares. Don't get me wrong I liked being ogled and admired, what girl wouldn't, but it had gotten worse as my banshee powers came into play.

Banshees were naturally beautiful women and became more so when they reached maturity. Lucky us... My classmates checked me out, their faces shifted and changed. Some peeked glimpses from under bangs, while others stared blatantly without a single regard. Teagan had already experienced the constant stares, glares, and jealousy from the whole student body; even the faculty couldn't keep their eyes off her.

It was now my turn to be the talk of the school and the envy of everyone around me. It might be cool for a few days, yet I didn't think I could handle too much attention. I hid behind my books as class rolled on. I couldn't wait until this day ended.

The black tabletops were cool against my warm skin. Sometimes I wished I could melt into the ceramic top or turn invisible at will. I looked over at Teagan for some guidance, but she just stared off into space, lost in her own thoughts again. I sighed. I had to deal with this on my own, I guess, since I knew Kaydynce wouldn't be of any help to me. I shifted my gaze over to her anyway. She was fluttering her eyelashes at some first-year boy who couldn't take his eyes off us.

I nudged her. "Kaydynce, stop messing with the poor boy you might give him a heart attack." She just laughed.

Kaydynce loved being a banshee and getting all of the attention from boys and girls alike. She reveled in her powers of seduction, but being half succubus might also cause that. Her mom was a banshee while her dad was an incubus. Weird combination if you ask me.

"You're overreacting. I'm just having a little fun, is all."

Her eyes twinkled while a smirk played across her pink lips. Kaydynce's finger glided over the boy's hand, which had crept closer to her.

I shook my head knowing I would never be able to drag her away from her flirting. Instead, I tried to concentrate on covalent bonding. I understood half of what Mr. Cole was saying before the bell rang for second period. Everyone rushed out of the room. Chairs scraped and shoes slapped against the tile. We were the last to leave, but before I could make it out the door Mr. Cole stopped me. Teagan and Kaydynce barely gave me a second glance before booking it like the rest of the class. I glared at their retreating forms. Worthless friends.

"Ms. Gray, may I have a word with you for a moment?"

I nodded, wondering what he wanted to talk to me about. I ambled back over to his desk, holding my books against my chest.

"Well, Ms. Gray, I've noticed a slight drop in your grade for this class. If you want to bring it up, surely, I can tutor you after school," he said casually.

He gave me a slow once-over, his lips curving up. I shivered, chills running up and down my spine. I knew that look. I could only assume what he meant by 'tutor me'. The offer was tempting. I did need a boost in my grade, and Mr. Cole wasn't bad looking for his age with his rich brown hair and dark green eyes. However he was in his forties, and I was only eighteen. Doing shit with my teacher was not on my list of things to do.

"No thank you, Mr. Cole, but I appreciate it the offer. I will try my best to do better."

I took a step toward the door. He grabbed my arm and yanked me back. The momentum sent me into his chest. My books flew out of my hands, scattering across the tiled floor. The heat of his hand seared my skin. I struggled, not believing this was happening.

My pulse raced, pounding in my ears. His grip tightened as he held my wrists together. I pulled against him. His breath stung my face. It smelled of coffee and loneliness. My heart thrashed against my sternum as I fought. I did the only thing I could think of. I kicked him square in the privates. He let go, crumbling to the ground. I sprinted to the door, hair falling into my face.

My body crashed into something solid and warm. Air rushed out of my lungs from the impact. My body flailed. Hands rested on my shoulders, steadying me. I didn't have time for this. I peeked back at Mr. Cole to see him getting up. I yelped, heart stopping for a moment. No, no, no! I pushed against the person, panic gripping my chest. Those same hands that had saved me from falling, tucked me behind his solid form. His palms were rough and calloused against my soft ones.

Odd. I peered up to find the guy I had seen in the hallway. My eyes widened at the realization.

"What's going on here?" the guy asked.

His voice was rough and deep like thunder. It made my body weak just hearing it.

I shook my head and tried to control this sudden feeling while peeking past his arm to where Mr. Cole stood.

"Nothing that concerns you, Mr. O'Neil, now why don't you run back to class and let Ms. Gray, and I finish our conversation," he replied, motioning his hand toward the door.

O'Neil? The name sounded familiar, but I didn't have time to worry about that now. I started to shake uncontrollably at just the thought of being alone with Mr. Cole again. I felt his eyes studying me, searing my skin. My breath hitched.

"Oh, I'll leave, but not without her."

His strong arms wrapped around my waist and led me away. His hand scorched my skin through my shirt. Just his touch sent waves of heat coursing through my body. I turned my head back to find Mr. Cole standing by the doorway glaring at me.

I should have reported it, I know, but I didn't. Despite his flaws Mr. Cole was a great teacher. I shook my head. I glanced up at my savior. He had red-brown hair that covered his ears and a lean but muscular build. His eyes found mine and raised a brow. His honey-colored eyes stunned me. The slow spread of a grin didn't help either.

Warmth crept up my cheeks as we continued to stare at each other, which probably wasn't the best idea when pushing through a crowded hallway. I tripped over my feet. His grip on my waist tightened, holding me against his body. I ducked my head down, embarrassed by his presence and the constant stares we got.

"Th-Thank you," I stuttered under my breath.

He stopped. The hair on the back on my neck stood on end. I didn't even have to see him to know his eyes were on me. Warm fingers touched under my chin and lifted it up. I met his gaze. Heat coursed between us. I gulped as I got lost in the pools of liquid gold.

"What happened back there?"

My lips trembled. "H-He wanted to bring my grade up... but not by tutoring"

"Oh," was all he said before jerking me against his chest, holding me tight.

I let myself relax into his arms feeling safe for the first time today. I should have pushed him away. Who was I to let a stranger hold me? I didn't know this person and yet there we were, locked in each other's arms. We stayed like that until the bell rang for second period to begin. The reaction I had to him left me confused. Was I just too traumatized? Was it because he had intervened? I wasn't sure what the answer was.

"Let me take you to the nurse's office," he said suddenly.

His arms scooped under my legs and lifted me to his chest. I blinked, mouth hanging agape. My body collapsed into his arms. The guy's muscles flexed with each step to the nurse's office. If it had been anyone else, I would have made a fuss, yet I felt safe in his presence.

It was a feeling I wasn't used to. Everything about him seemed familiar—from his golden eyes to the sound of his deep, rumbling voice. I was lolled into a sense of calm as his arms rocked me back and forth. I must have dozed off because the next thing I knew I was sitting up in one of the nurse's beds gasping for air.

"Shh, it's all right now. You're safe here," a feminine voice said, pushing me back into a reclining position.

I had been dreaming of a boy with honey-colored eyes. I had known him long ago, but he had left, breaking my heart. I shook my head. I regarded the room with its white walls and posters of diseases and infections. I shuddered just seeing them. This wasn't a place I wanted to be at all. I cast my eyes around until I spotted my savior, giving him a small smile.

"Hi," I said a little groggily.

"Hello to you, too." A grin played across his lips, lips that seemed to tempt me.

"How long have I been asleep?"

"I'd say you've been asleep for maybe thirty minutes or so," he replied, "but don't worry I told the nurse to let all of your teachers know that you weren't feeling good."

I raised a brow. *Interesting,* I thought, as I checked him out once more.

"So, what shall I call you since I don't think savior would be the best thing?" I asked playfully, surprising myself.

"Kaelin O'Neil," he said, but there was something about the way he said it, like it was an inside joke that I should have been a part of. Weird.

I knew that name, have always known that name yet it had been so long since I had heard it.

"Oh my god, Kaelin, it's Aislin, Aislin Gray. We used to go to school together before you moved."

My heart thrashed and clawed at my chest. I couldn't believe he was here and had saved me. The boy I had known had grown into himself. He wasn't all arms and legs anymore. Kaelin's smile widened.

"Oh, I know." He chuckled. "But I will say you have grown since the last time I saw you," he joked, giving me a slow once over that made my skin tingle. Had I?

Happiness fluttered through me. The horror of the day dissipated.

"When did you get back? I haven't seen you in any of my classes, so it had to have been recent, right?"

"Actually, I got back yesterday." His eyes danced in the off-white lights.

"Oh, well then that means you need someone to show you around the town again since you've been away for so long," I said flirtatiously. The town has changed in three years...right?

His golden eyes lit up; a broad smile spread across his face.

"That sounds like a plan." He held out his hand.

I blushed and took it. His fingers wrapped around mine and helped me out of the bed. We smiled at each other and strolled out of the nurse's office.

The halls were barren, not a soul in sight. Kaelin guided us through the double doors to the parking lot. A gust of wind whipped past me, sending strands of my hair into his face. I giggled, covering my mouth. His golden eyes narrowed right before quick fingers danced across my sides. I screamed then giggled, thrashing away from him. Kaelin smirked. My heart skipped a beat. It was like old times, joking and laughing together. I had missed this.

"Do you remember sneaking out and stealing your mom's car just to see me even though you had been grounded for a week?" I asked as we walked.

Kaelin's grin widened, golden eyes dancing. "Yeah, I was grounded for two whole months after that, but it had been worth it." His shoulder nudged mine. "If I remember correctly that was also the night you snuck a bottle of wine out of your mom's liqueur cabinet."

I laughed. "That was horrible wine."

"That was a vintage 1971 Mosel-Saar-Ruwer Riesling. It was an excellent choice except for the fact that we were only fifteen." He held up a pinky and puckered his lips.

I rolled my eyes. Those were the best days of my childhood. It felt like ages since I had seen him. He had been my shoulder to cry on when I was sad, my encouragement when I didn't believe in myself, and the one I had hoped would be there always. Up until the day he left.

"So why did you come back?" I asked, nudging his shoulder back.

He stopped and turned toward me, golden eyes searching my face. His sun-kissed cheek reddened. Kaelin opened his mouth then closed it. I watched with one brow raised, waiting.

His Adam's apple bobbed before words left his lips or rather one word. "You."

I froze, heart stuck in my throat. He said it so seriously that I was caught off guard. We had been friends since we were little, but I had never expected him to feel anything more than friendship for me. I laughed and jostled his shoulder.

"No, be serious, Kaelin."

The look in his golden eyes said something else entirely. They smoldered, sending shivers down my spine. I still couldn't believe that Kaelin had come back. He was the same old goofy boy that I had known all my life. Could he truly have feelings for me? Was I that blind? I shook my head. He stepped closer and raised a hand toward my cheek. I gulped, bile rising as a pain shot through me.

My throat tingled and closed as my vision blurred. *Not now, please...* I knew then that it was about to start, my first Death Call. The asphalt wavered in front of me. Ice slid down my back, chilling the heat I had once felt. I closed my eyes wishing it would go away. Wishes rarely ever came true, though. An ear-splitting screech erupted from my lips as my eyesight turned into a vision of death. I held my head. The premonition played out, and then just like that it was over. I crumbled to the ground. Tears streaked down my pale cheeks.

"Aislin, what's wrong?" Kaelin asked. His voice was muffled.

Rocks crunched in front of me. Feather light touches on my arms signaled he was right there. I now understood Teagan's bitterness and what my mom hadn't told me. My Death Call had been of the last person I had ever expected, and the one person I had fallen for. Again. The one I had always loved—I had seen the death of Kaelin Quinn O'Neil, my first love.

# Chapter 2

"Aislin, please tell me what's wrong."

I shook my head. I couldn't tell him of the horrors I had just seen, especially since they involved him. I wanted to scream at the world at how unfair this was. I had found him again, and now the universe was going to take him away. Fuck that! I pushed myself up and ran. My shaky legs couldn't hold me. I fell, tripping over my feet, and crashed to the pavement.

My hands skidded on the gravel. Rocks sliced through my palms. I winced. Kaelin was close behind. I could hear his heavy breathing and footsteps pounding against the pavement. I lay there with unshed tears blurring my vision until Kaelin reached me. He scooped me up into his arms without a word and strode toward his blue, beat-up pickup truck. I didn't say a word.

My head rested against his still beating heart. He opened the passenger's door, rust falling lightly on my head. Kaelin set me down in the seat. It squished under me—worn leather. His truck smelled of old leather and the woods in autumn. It smelled like him. A single tear escaped.

Memories flashed through my mind:

*"Is this it?" I asked.*

*"What? You don't like her?"*
*I bit my lip, studying the blue, rusted pickup truck. It was an old Chevy with paint chipping off the hood and sides. "You sure it won't break down on us?"*
*Kaelin laughed.*

*"Do you trust me?"*

*I held his golden gaze. "Completely."*

*He smiled, picking me up. I squealed as he spun me around. He stopped and held me like a football as he opened the passenger-side door. Flakes of rust rained down on us. We both laughed.*

That was the day he got his truck and infused it with his smell. I didn't know if I could handle being around him, surrounded by his scent, all the while knowing that he would die soon. I didn't know when it would happen, yet I knew death waited for an opportunity to strike.

We rode in silence with me balled up in the passenger's seat, hollow eyes cast down at my shoes. I felt his hand, feather light, touch mine. I cringed away like I had been bitten. He backed off with a sigh probably thinking I was psychotic or something. Before I even had to think how he knew where I lived, we were entering my driveway.

"Thanks," I muttered as I opened the door and got out of his truck.

I had made it to the steps before I felt a hand on my shoulder. I could feel the heat from his palm through my blue blouse. Just his touch made me all warm and tingly. I shrugged it off, not wanting anymore contact than I had to. The closer I got, the harder it would be to do the inevitable.

"Aislin, wait. I just wanted to wish you a happy birthday."

I winced. That was the icing on the cake. Shit. I had completely forgotten that it was my birthday after the whole Mr. Cole incident, and now this... This had to be one of the worst birthdays I had ever had, almost being sexually assaulted by a teacher, and then getting my first Death Call? I almost broke down in front of him, yet I was saved as my front door opened, revealing my grandma. She glanced from me to Kaelin then ushered me inside without a single word. Kaelin was left just standing there on my porch, mouth hanging open, words never forming.

"Cassidy," my grandma called, "can you usher this boy off our property?"

My mom ran down the stairs and out the door in a flash. I heard her talking through the open door.

"I'm sorry, but you must leave. My daughter apologizes and thanks you, but I think we can handle it from here."

I sighed, knowing I would have to deal with the same problems tomorrow, but I had other things to deal with now. I could hear his sneakers scuffing against my steps as he shuffled away, no doubt with his head hung low. The minute my mom entered the house again I attacked.

"How could you? I can't believe you didn't tell me!" I screamed, glaring straight at my mom. "You're not getting off easy either, Grandma," I growled, turning to glare at my grandma's retreating form.

I still couldn't believe that they both didn't tell me who my first Death Call would be. I think I had a right to know that I would see the death of my first and only love.

"Sweetheart, it's not like that." My mom fidgeted with her hands, looking back and forth between my grandma and me. "We couldn't tell you. It's part of our code to let the young ones find out on their own. It's what makes us banshees. We are keening women who mourn the loss of someone dear to us while seeing the death of others."

"How am I supposed to go to school knowing that he is going to die at any moment?" I said, balling up my fists, not understanding how this could be happening to me.

I paced around the room, running my hands through my hair.

"You must cut all ties with him it will help to soften the blow when it finally happens," my grandma said, her voice carrying from the kitchen.

I knew what she was saying was true, yet I didn't know if I could. How do I cut ties with someone I've known almost all my life? There would be no easy way out.

"She's right, you know. Mother always knows best. Though it may hurt at first, time heals all wounds," my mom said.

She grabbed ahold of my wrist and stopped my pacing long enough to embrace me. I hugged her back knowing they were both right. Still... the thought of not seeing Kaelin again ripped a hole in my chest. She let go and smiled. It didn't meet her big midnight-blue eyes. My mom and I looked alike. We both had the same dark brown hair and pale skin, yet our eyes were a different shade of blue. I had pale blue eyes like my dad while she had dark blue eyes that sometimes seemed black.

"Well, I think I'm going to head off to bed it's been a very long day," I sighed.

My grandma gave a loud cough. I stopped, hand inches away from the banister and turned to see my mom with her big puppy dog eyes and pouty lips. I groaned.

"Awe, but, sweetheart, I'm throwing you a birthday party. You can't miss that." She fluttered her eyelashes. "I invited all of your friends from school."

I let out a breath, rolling my eyes. There was no way I was going to be able to get out of it especially since my mom loved throwing parties. She loved parties so much she started a business called Party Time. I know, not very original, but it works. I hadn't noticed before, but the air was filled with the scent of nutmeg and vanilla. My only guess was that my mom or grandma was baking a cake. Was I that distraught that I didn't notice?

A knock at the door had both of us turning. I glared at my mom. She shrugged, her face crinkling as she smiled. I rushed up the stairs that were across from the front door. The stairs were white like everything else in the house except my room, which was sky blue.

I was the only one who had wanted a splash of color in their life. My house happened to be the only white house on my street. All the other houses were brick red, brown, or a darker hue. There weren't many other differences besides our house having a substantial amount of backyard and woods combined. We were the last house on the block, the dead-end.

I needed to find something flattering to wear, though I knew it wouldn't matter much. I would still be the center of attention. The thought of my whole class at my house sent my heart thrashing to escape. My legs wobbled as I entered my room. I stared at the colored wall with the few posters I had hung up. In the center of the room, against the back wall sat my queen-sized bed. The blue pillows and comforter were neatly tucked in, though I knew I had left it in disarray this morning.

To the right, sat my vanity painted eggshell white to offset the blue. I sighed. All I wanted to do was curl up and cry my eyes out. Maybe I could close my eyes for a minute or two. It was common to be fashionably late to your own party, right? I plopped face down into my pillows and breathed in the floral laundry detergent. The bed sunk slowly under my weight. Its softness made me compliant. Everything in me relaxed under its comfort and familiarity. The corner of my mouth lifted in a half-smile. This was what I wanted. To not be bothered and be able to come to terms with things on my own. That was fair, right?

The warmth of the comforter had me drifting in a sort of out of body experience. I was weightless and free. The world dissolved around me until it was just clouds of soft whites and greys. No responsibilities, no death or life, just being a part of the sky. The problem with astral projection, though, is when you snap back, everything comes crashing down with you.

"Aislin!"

I gasped, sitting up. My room refocused in my vision as I blinked. What the hell? A heaviness settled over my body. I shivered, goosebumps prickling my arms. The last things I remembered barreled through my head. I winced then groaned. My party...

I stumbled out of bed and stared at the array of clothes in my closet. I searched through the many shirts, dresses, skirts, and jeans that were hanging up until I finally found something I liked. It was a tight, low-cut, royal-purple dress that barely covered my bottom but showed off what curves I had. It had sleeves that scarcely covered my shoulders. It was a quite simple and elegant dress. When I put it on, I was satisfied. Just for a little modesty, I slipped on black, fishnet leggings. Next step, my hair.

My long, brown hair hung loosely down my back, plain and boring. I needed to spice it up a bit. I went to my vanity, sat down and checked myself out in the mirror. What would look good? Curls would offset my face. I nodded to myself and picked up the curling iron that sat on top. I turned it on, and while I waited for it to warm up, I opened my makeup kit.

I browsed through the different shades until I came upon a deep purple that would go perfectly with my dress. With a swipe of the brush, both lids were covered. My lips curved up as I swished on a light pink blush to my cheeks. Any color would help my pale skin. I blinked at myself in the mirror. A hollowness had settled in my eyes that no makeup could hide. A nagging feeling hit my stomach. Something was about to happen...

I shook my head and applied liner to my bottom lids. Nothing too fancy. I didn't think siren or cat eyes would do anything. My insides curled and twisted like roots trying to latch on. I just needed to calm my nerves. I took a deep breath then let it go slowly. Today was to celebrate my birth, nothing more.

I picked up my curling iron and tried not to think of all the people that were starting to show up. And all eyes waiting for me to make an appearance. I set the curling iron down and studied my handy work. My chocolate brown curls bounced around my face as I moved my head to make sure I had gotten every spot. I got up slowly, satisfied, and went back over to my closet to pick out the perfect shoes.

I settled on a pair of black heels that wrapped around my ankles and calves then walked out of my room to the daunting stairs. I picked my way slowly down making sure I didn't fall and make a fool of myself. As soon as I took the last step, I heard whistles and cheers aimed straight at me. I sauntered into my living room to find the whole room packed with sweaty bodies as they pressed against each other.

"Happy Birthday, Aislin!" A cheer went out saying my name over and over again until that was all I could hear.

Everyone cleared a path as I passed. I smiled awkwardly as I strode through the crowd and felt light taps and heard happy birthdays from every person that I passed. Ugh, I couldn't believe my mom had done this. The whole house was covered in blue and purple streamers and balloons that said happy birthday all over them. In the amount of time it took to get ready, my mom had decorated. I could have sworn the house had been empty of streamers and balloons.

"All right, everyone, it's party time. Everyone through the backdoor and let's get this party started!" Mom yelled from the kitchen.

The crowd rushed out of the room in a flash, dragging me along with it. I followed them out into my backyard, which had been decorated with Japanese lanterns and lines of Christmas lights strung up across our patio. I smiled. I had to admit mom had done well. The place was amazing. My mom had even gotten a real DJ who was sitting in the corner with his CDs beside him.

"Aislin, oh my God, your mom is incredible. I can't believe she did all of this by herself!" Kaydynce squealed, running up behind me and hugging me with a death grip.

"Yeah, I know," I said, peeling her off me.

Her grip was strong. It was like detaching a leach.

"So, I heard you got your first Death Call." She waggled her eyebrows at me. "How was it?" I opened my mouth then closed it. "Oh my God, I bet it was awesome. I can't wait to get mine," she said with stars in her eyes.

She gazed longingly for a moment before snapping back to reality. Ugh, I didn't know what to tell her. I couldn't tell her the truth according to my mom since it was "against the code."

"Yeah, it was amazing," I said sarcastically, hoping she would get it, but of course she was too delusional to even pay attention to the way I said it. All she heard was, "It was amazing."

"What was amazing?"

My heart sank as I recognized that voice. Just the sound of his deep, raspy voice made my heart speed up and my skin tingle. My gut had been warning me, but I hadn't heeded it. Now I had to face the one person I was hoping to avoid, Kaelin.

# Chapter 3

"Aislin had her first— Ow," Kaydynce yelped, rubbing her arm. I threw daggers her way.

"Had her first what?" he asked Kaydynce, raising a brow at me.

My body felt like it was on fire as his eyes roamed down it with a small smile playing across his lips. His golden eyes were twinkling with hidden mischief as he waited for her reply. Kaydynce hadn't glanced his way until that moment. She turned, eyes widening.

"Kaelin, oh my God! It's so good to see you!" she squealed, running and hugging him. He picked her up and swung her around playfully.

"It's good to see you too, Kay," he laughed, putting her down and mussing up her short blond hair.

Something rose inside of me at the sight of them together. A pain stabbed through my chest. I had completely forgotten that they used to date, and she had treated him like hell. He would never see it like that though.

She had used her seductive ability to play with his mind for "fun" she would say. The worst part was that she had known that I liked him at the time, and she still went for him. He couldn't resist her either. It's part of what made a succubus so powerful. No one could resist her.

Was I angry at him? No. Yet, I couldn't help the bitterness that lingered on my tongue. I couldn't even make myself hate Kaydynce. We were both young still, barely in our teen years, new to the prospect of romance. Teagan held onto it for me, though. Forgiveness was not something she gave easily.

I left them like that. The image of them together burned into my retinas. I slipped away to a shaded, secluded area where I wouldn't be bothered. It was one of the bigger trees on the outskirts of the woods. The rest of the woods were to my back, whispering with the wind. The darkness shielded me from the lights of the lanterns strewn across the yard. The sun cast its last rays through the branches. I sighed as I heard the rustle of leaves and muffled footsteps.

"Hey, why aren't you dancing with everyone else, sweetheart?" Mom asked, taking a seat beside me. Her eyes searched mine, a frown marring her lips.

I leaned my head against the trunk and studied the darkening sky. "I just kind of want to be alone right now, is all."

She nodded, not pushing the issue. "All right, when you are ready, come join the fun before it ends. I would hate to have thrown this party for you, and you not have any fun," she said, before skipping off to join the party again.

She disappeared among the crowd, blending in. It didn't take long for him to find me again. His brown hair blew in the light breeze as he walked over to where I sat. He wore a button-up, black shirt and khaki pants with a broad smile spreading across his lips.

"I found you," he said, as he reached my spot.

"I guess you have," I said back, staring up at the stars again.

Kaelin sat beside me. "Why did you run off like that?"

I closed my eyes and tried to think of other things besides his close proximity. His scent swirled around me.

"It seemed like you and Kaydynce were having a good time together, and I didn't want to ruin it, so I left," I said, though only speaking half the truth.

The real reason was I was jealous of them, wishing I could have what they had even for a moment, but that would never happen after what I had seen. Kaelin would be out of my life soon enough so why should it matter if Kaydynce and him got back together. Yet a part of me still wanted the chance to have something more than friendship with him even if it was fleeting. Was that so bad, to want something I could never have?

"Is that jealousy I hear in your voice?" he joked, nudging my shoulder lightly.

A small smile played across my lips.

"Of course not, don't be absurd," I replied, pushing him back.

He laughed, nudging me again until I finally pushed him for real and ran off. I didn't know why, I just did, but it made me feel like a little kid again, joking and laughing. He chased after me as I darted through the trees glancing back at him every once and a while to see how close he was.

When I didn't see him anymore, I paused, panic fluttering through my chest. He jumped out of the bushes beside me and wrapped his arms around my waist.

"Gotcha," he whispered. His breath tickled the back of my neck.

"It seems you have," I chuckled, shivering against the warmth of his body.

I tilted my head up. My vision filled with his honey-brown eyes. If I gazed into them for too long, I'd get lost. His lips spread into a grin. I gulped, heart fluttering. Kaelin's body shifted against me. His arm tightened as one of his hands tipped my head back further. My breath hitched, lips parting. He leaned in, nose brushing mine. My eyelids closed on their own.

A light pressure fell onto my lips, soft and warm. I melted into his touch. A breath shared between us. A hunger burned, wanting to sweep me off my feet. I broke the kiss first and stumbled backwards. His arms fell away. My fingers touched my lips.

"I-I can't do this," I said, shaking my head. Tears collected and fell like raindrops.

I turned and ran, not looking back to see his face. Branches reached out and snagged in my hair, trying to stop me. I couldn't go back there, not with him. It would be so easy to let go and let my feelings take over, but I knew I couldn't do that, not if I wanted to keep my heart whole. It felt like my heart was already breaking just from our brief encounters. The softness of lips still lingered on mine.

"Aislin!" he called. His own fumbling footsteps followed my every step. Grunts and hisses echoed through the darkened woods.

I ran even faster trying to rid myself of him. Just his presence made me weak. It felt like he was a lingering part in my body that I could never purge myself of. The woods were eerie and sinister in the starlight. The night air grew chillier the longer I ran, though it should have been the other way around. My breath fogged in front of my face. Goosebumps rose on my arms at the temperature drop.

"He is going to die," someone whispered against my ear, sending chills down my spine.

I stopped and glanced around myself frantically, but there was no one in sight. I shook my head. It was nothing.

"He is going to die. Because of you," someone else whispered, brushing up against my arm. I jumped.

"Who are you?" I called out into the darkness.

I waited for a reply but only heard a cackling laugh and someone sobbing. My whole body froze as apparitions appeared out of thin air. Deadpan eyes, wispy white hair, and bodies made of nothingness. I had never seen one though I knew they existed just like every other supernatural being.

"Why are you here?" I asked, my voice catching in a sudden gust of wind.

"He is going to die, and become one of us," one of them said and laughed.

Its laugh was like nails on a chalkboard. My hair stood up on the back of my neck and arms as they floated closer to me. I had heard stories about ghosts, Thevshi in Irish, spirits that couldn't leave the earthly plane because of affection, anger, or an unfinished duty.

Though they seemed harmless they had the power to possess people in their anger. They are called poltergeists now. They crowded in closer to me and then they were gone like a snap of the finger, poof. Dread filled my insides. Ghosts were rarely scared off, unless... I scanned the darkened forest until I noticed something creeping toward me. I could barely see it as it blended into the darkness.

I shuddered as I saw what had scared the Thevshis away, a dark mass almost as tall as myself with dark tendrils flying off its cloak. It was faceless. My heart raced as I recognized this being from tales my mom used to tell me. I was face to face with a wraith. It seemed like it could swallow me whole. I gulped, petrified, as I waited for it to make its move. I knew I shouldn't be afraid, I had nothing to fear. Wraiths did the same thing as banshees but try telling that to my racing heart.

The woods were quiet around us, like it held its breath, waiting for someone to make the first move. The silence only added to my fear as I tried to find an escape route. I knew it was futile. You can't outrun an apparition. I saw a bony hand rise out of the wraith's cloak from the corner of my eye. When I stared at it, I noticed that it was pointing straight at me. Not a good sign. There was a searing pain. I crumbled to my knees, holding my head as the vision played out in front of me.

*"Please, don't go," Kaydynce pleaded, staring up at him with her big blue eyes begging him not to leave.*

*She picked up her sheet and wrapped it around her naked body as she sat up on her bed. Her short, blond hair was mussed up like she had just woken up or other things. Her cheeks were flushed yet there was a slight pout to her lips.*

*He adjusted his pants and picked up his shirt from off the floor. "This is wrong, Kay, I shouldn't even be here, not with you."*

*Kaelin didn't even look at her as he put on his shirt, shoulders hunched.*

"*She turned you down, Kaelin. She doesn't want you, but I do, so please come back to bed,*" *she said, getting up and sauntering over to him.*

*The sheets slowly fell off her body to pool at her feet. He tensed, pain reflected in his golden eyes. Kaydynce touched his arm lightly. He shivered then pushed her away.*

"*She can't do for you what I can!*" *Kaydynce screamed, throwing a pillow at his retreating form.*

*He left Kaydynce's house and walked into the night. Kaelin shook his head, shoulders slumping even more. He had stormed out during Aislin's party and ran into Kaydynce.*

*He had left with her without meaning to. He had planned on just leaving, but she had a sort of allure to her that made him reconsider. A sigh escaped his lips. He ran a hand through his hair. Kaelin shuffled down the barely lit street with his head hung low and a hand in his pocket. His other hand dragged down his face before balling up into a fist. He continued to walk not noticing the shadow following close behind him. A pale, fragile hand grabbed his head and tilted it to the side. He struggled, trying to break the grip yet nothing seemed to work. The grip was too strong.*

*The attacker was a woman with white hair that fell in soft ringlets all the way down her back. She kissed his neck lightly. Lips of red coaxed him to relax. He stopped struggling, just long enough for her pearly fangs to sink into his neck. She took her time draining him dry. Purrs emanated from her throat. When she finished, she let him go and sauntered away. His lifeless body crashed to the ground; golden eyes vacant. She didn't even take the time to clean up her mess.*

# Chapter 4

I heard myself scream in anger and despair as the vision came to an end. Tears streamed down my face, as my life crumbled around me. I had changed the vision... I... oh, God...

"Aislin," he called in the distance, his voice rising in pitch. I closed my eyes and allowed my heart to shatter into pieces.

I had changed the events that would lead to his death just by turning him down. My mind was blown as I thought of the many possibilities that could happen just by me doing or not doing something. I guess what they say is true, "Actions speak louder than words."

"Aislin, where are you? Please answer me!"

I didn't acknowledge his calls and just waited for him to find me. I knew he would, he always did. It didn't take him long to push through the bushes and tree branches to find me on my knees with my legs spread out beside me. I couldn't look at him not when I knew where he would be once I turned him down again. Yet I didn't want to reject him. I didn't even want to avoid him. All I wanted was him at that moment.

I couldn't deny my feelings for him anymore, especially now that I knew I could change his fate. I was still a little angry that Kaydynce would try to take him away from me... again. We had been friends since we were little you would think that would mean something to her, but of course not. *Best friend my ass.* I wiped away the tears that hadn't fallen yet.

"Aislin, are you all right?" Kaelin asked. He kneeled beside me, eyes searching my face. "Did you fall or hurt your ankle?"

"I'm fine, just a little shaken. I thought I saw something, and it scared me," I said, getting up slowly and turned around to face him.

He picked himself up off the ground and studied my face once more. "Why'd you run away?"

His golden eyes held so much hurt in them that I couldn't speak. I couldn't fathom why he would appear so wounded. It felt surreal to see him actually showing an interest in me.

I mean sure I had always envisioned it would happen, that someday we would fall madly in love with each other yet that was only a fantasy. Though I should have known better. All fantasies have a hint of truth in them just like legends and myths.

"I-I, um . . ." I couldn't think of a good enough excuse. It was like my mind had a brain-fart, and no words could be found. "You, um, shocked me. I didn't expect it and, um, yeah that's the best I have."

He shook his head and started laughing. I frowned at his reaction. What was so funny?

"So pretty much what you're saying is that you got scared of what was happening between us, and you ran, am I right?"

I nodded, eyes widening at his quick deduction. Heat coursed up my cheeks. Usually, guys weren't that perceptive. He was more intuitive than I gave him credit for, which meant I had to be even more on guard unless I wanted to let out the biggest secret to the human race, the paranormal are real. Though we try to keep it a secret somehow certain paranormal beings have been caught and to be found quite real like vampires for instance.

It's kind of hard to hide vampires, as they tend to leave pretty significant bite marks on their victims plus, they always seem to leave a trail of dead bodies behind. It's not hard to put the pieces together even a dim human could presume that vampires are real. They were the main culprits for serial killers. Though I knew it shouldn't matter since in the end, he would die so there was no point in trying to hide yet a lifetime of secrecy made me cautious.

He stepped toward me until we were inches apart. If I wanted to, I could lean in and feel his warmth. "Why are you so afraid?" he whispered. Simple words yet they send my heart pounding into overtime.

He studied me with his knowing eyes catching every little itch and fidget I made. It was like he was studying a book for hidden meanings in its words. I nibbled on my bottom lip.

"I . . ." I didn't know what to tell him. Should I tell him the truth? Yet if I did, I might lose him anyways. What was the right decision? I sucked in a breath and made my decision.

"Kaelin, I'm afraid because I know you're going to—." A loud commotion just a few yards away interrupted me.

We both rushed over to find Kaydynce kissing some boy; however, that didn't seem to be the cause of the commotion. The noise was coming from a girl huddled up against a tree. She was screaming for Kaydynce to stop, saying she was killing him. She was a lithe, pixie-like girl with long brown hair and dark green eyes.

I knew who she was, yet I couldn't place her name. I knew she was some kind of fey, someone who could feel a persons' life force. This wasn't a good sign. If I didn't end this now Kaydynce would expose us all, especially since a crowd had started to gather. I acted. I had heard that a feeding succubus was very strong and that they don't like to be disturbed.

"Kaydynce, stop," I said, rushing over and tried to break them apart.

I could see the boy's body twitch as she slowly drained him. I had to act now and fast before it was too late. I searched around for something that could somehow end this mess. Sighing, I reeled back my right hand and let it fall, swiping Kaydynce on her right cheek so hard that she momentarily faltered. A red handprint spread across her cheek. The crowd gasped. Shit. It was enough for me to get in between her and her victim.

"Please, you need to stop before you kill the poor boy," I whispered, hoping she would listen to reason so that we could get out of this mess.

She hissed at me. Her blue eyes glowing eerily as she let me know that I had disturbed her. Oh shit. I now had to deal with a pissed off succubus, which mind you wasn't the best place to be. I was between her and her meal. Grinding my teeth, I stood my ground, showing her I wasn't afraid.

She hissed at me again and tried to get around me to the now passed out boy who was as pale as a ghost. I slapped her again. The crowd went wild, chanting "Fight! Fight!". This time it knocked her out of her feeding frenzy. She blinked a few times frowning before her eyes seemed to focus on her surroundings. She rubbed her cheek where a second red handprint had formed.

"W-What happened?" she asked, staring from me to the crowd that had gathered around us.

I nodded toward the boy lying across the tree roots behind me. Her eyes bugged out in horror as she saw the unconscious boy whose skin had turned deathly pale. She had almost killed him because she didn't have the control to stop. She had almost exposed paranormal beings to the world. I wrapped an arm around her and drew her close then led her away from prying eyes though all anybody wanted to see was the unconscious boy.

"He got overexcited," I said as an excuse so I could lead Kaydynce away without students asking questions. A few awes and boos sounded behind us. The fight was over. A couple classmates mumbled about it being over a boy. They weren't wrong.

Kaelin followed after us like a lost puppy though I knew he wanted answers too. He had that determined expression on his face like nothing was going to stop him from finding out the truth. I didn't like it. It would lead to all hell breaking loose if he ever found out. He was already superstitious, but that was to be expected from a descendant of an Irishman. The Irish folk were naturally superstitious since superstition ruled Ireland as a king ruled England.

I led Kaydynce far enough away from the crowd so that we had complete privacy besides the stubborn Kaelin. She stumbled beside me, holding on tight as her feet faltered. Anybody else besides my kin and me would think she was drunk though she probably was with most of that boy's life force in her body. Her heels dragged against the ground, as her body grew sluggish. She was only part succubus so feeding as much as she did made her more vulnerable than strong like most succubae. I set her down against a tree and knelt beside her.

"Kay, you have to wake up. You can't rest here, not now. I need you to wake up so we can have a little chat," I said, shaking her shoulders and lightly tapping her cheeks yet nothing seemed to wake her from her deep slumber.

I sighed, sitting back and resting my head against the other side of the tree trunk as wariness washed over me like a wave. At least if she woke now, she wouldn't immediately see me. I was so tired and worn out. I had aged in less than a day with everything that had happened.

"I'm guessing she is pretty much dead to the world at the moment," Kaelin said, looking over at Kaydynce on the other side of the tree and took a seat beside me.

"Yeah, I don't think anything can wake her up, and I'd rather not be here when she wakes. She is going to have a nasty hangover and will probably be very grouchy," I replied.

Kaelin laughed, his laughter lit up his face and eyes so much so that he shone like the sun. I craved that sunlight that seemed to warm me from the inside out. It felt like I had been cold all my life just waiting for this warmth to find me.

"What? Is there something on my face?" he asked playfully, noticing my intense stare yet he stared right back not withholding anything.

I could see it all written plainly on his face, no matter what, he wasn't going to give up on me even if I rejected him. His golden eyes turned to molten gold as his stare intensified. I could feel the heat coming off of him and I saw a multitude of emotions flash through his gaze as it darkened. I couldn't say no, not this time.

"I don't know about—," he cut me off with a kiss so gentle, but it held so much emotion that it brought tears to my eyes. He cupped my face tenderly with his hands. They grew rougher as his passion and lust pushed through. I didn't stop him. Instead, I added my own passion, pressing closer to him never wanting this moment to end. Nothing lasts forever. I knew the consequences of my actions, yet I wouldn't change it for the world. I finally knew what true love was. I would never let it go. I knew if I didn't though, I would lose my heart in the process.

# Chapter 5

I woke up suddenly with my heart thumping against my chest as bile rose up my throat. I scanned my surroundings, trying to calm my thrashing heart. I was still in the woods, not alone though. *It was only a dream,* I told myself, but it had seemed so real. I had lost him forever in my dream. It was like he had vanished from this earth leaving nothing behind.

Just the thought of losing him made my heart constrict and beat even faster. It shouldn't affect me. I knew he would die eventually. Death is inevitable. I couldn't fathom not having him around though. It would be even harder the closer I got to him, yet I didn't want to stop.

Kaelin's soft breathing filled my ears. His arm, slung over my waist, tightened. I smiled, studying his sleeping form. I nuzzled closer to him and wondered how this had happened. I remembered his gentle then rough kisses against my lips, his hands branding my skin, and his deep, sensual whispers.

*I guess we fell asleep,* I thought as I touched my swollen lips. They were sore from the forcefulness of his lips pressing against mine, but I didn't mind, though my mother would if she ever found out. I knew they were only trying to protect me, yet life is full of risks, and I wanted to take all of them with Kaelin.

I knew it was irrational to want to spend the rest of my life with Kaelin, yet it felt like he was a part of me, and I was a part of him. The concept seemed unfathomable, but I knew it in my heart that it was true. He's my soul mate. I had heard the term used before, yet I had never conceived that it could ever happen to me, but it had. He stirred beside me. I turned my body in his arms to find him smiling like a fool.

"What?" I asked, studying his chiseled face.

"I'm surprised you're still here." I blinked and raised a brow. "I mean I'm glad you are it's just I had expected you to run the first chance you got," he replied, with a mischievous grin that lit up his face.

I hadn't seen him this happy in years, not since the day I met him. It felt like decades since that first meeting, and I hadn't really changed a bit, yet he had. He had finally gotten rid of his boyish features, and now he was a boy grown into a man. A sexy man at that with his chiseled face, six pack abs, and muscular arms. He had the body of a Greek god.

"Oh," was all I could think to say as I ran my hands down his arms and chest, mesmerized. He had taken his shirt off at some point during the night and wrapped it around my shoulders as a sort of blanket. I had never imagined that I could ever possibly snare a guy like him, others maybe but not him. He was too perfect, and I knew it could never last even if I didn't have the ability of Death Calling.

"Yeah, but I'm glad you stayed," he said, drawing me closer and planting a gentle kiss on my lips.

His lips were warm and soft. The combination sent chills down my arms and back.

"I should probably go. My mom is probably worried sick by now," I said, unwrapping his arms from around me and giving back his shirt.

I straightened my dress out as it had ridden up and gotten a little wrinkly from sleeping in it.

"Awe, can't you stay a little bit longer," he teased, his eyes shining. I smiled, shaking my head.

"If I stay any longer, I won't want to leave, and you know that," I joked though it was actually true.

"Oh, I know," he said, with a wink then grabbed for me.

I dodged his hands, laughing. He tried again, but this time he grabbed me around the waist dragging me back down with him. I squirmed in his arms, laughing, and turned to stare up at him. He smiled down at me, tightening his grip to make sure I didn't run.

"Kaelin, I can't stay," I whispered, as he leaned closer, cupping my cheek.

Reality was slowly sinking in. This wasn't a fairytale where there were happily ever after's, instead it was real life where nothing was ever perfect. I couldn't pretend that everything was going to be okay. I just couldn't, not when I knew the outcome.

"Please, just a little longer then we can pretend like this never happened," he said mournfully.

I was shocked by his response. The Kaelin I knew wouldn't have given up so easily on something or someone he wanted.

"Kaelin, that's not what I meant," I said, surprised.

*Is that the impression I gave off?* I asked myself, thinking back on how I acted. Did he think that it was just a fling, that I didn't really want him?

"Isn't it?" he accused, his mood souring.

I couldn't believe what I was hearing. Did he think I was really that shallow? I couldn't remember a time in my life that I had just fooled around then pretended like it never happened. My anger peaked at the accusation he had just made. I roughly pushed out of his arms and stood up. I was just going to walk away, but my anger got the best of me. I turned around to glare at him.

"I can't believe you would accuse me of-of being a tease!" I yelled, hurt that he would ever think that way of me.

He wasn't the Kaelin I had fallen for or the one that had been my best friend since kindergarten. Who was this guy? My heart clenched.

"Ais, wait, I didn't mean it like that," he pleaded, getting up and tried to catch my arm.

I wrenched away wishing I could just disappear.

"Then how did you mean it, Kaelin?" I asked, throwing my hands into the air and glared back at him. "Please clarify for me so that I can understand." I really didn't want to hear his explanation.

I was done, done with him, and done with this situation. So stupid... At this point I was so angry and hurt that I didn't care if he lived or died. He regarded me then cast his eyes down, ashamed. I knew he didn't have another explanation or meaning to what he had said. I turned away in disgust. I couldn't be here any longer not near him or in these woods.

I walked away from him, never looking back because I knew if I did, I would go back to him. I had finally given into my feelings and what did I get in return? Accusations that weren't justifiable. The world around me was lighting up with brilliant blues, pinks, and oranges as the sun crept up the sky yet my world was full of darkness. I hated how my world was full of sorrow and death. Just once I would like to be happy, but even my happiness was filled with mourning. I just couldn't get a break. No matter what I did my happiness was like a wisp of a thought that I couldn't capture.

He called after me; his voice echoing through the trees begging me to come back. I ignored it all. I ignored the voices whispering for me to go to him, the little brown eyes begging me to turn around, and even the trees that snagged on my dress trying to block my path.

Everything tried to tell me to turn around, to go back to him. I was being stupid and stubborn, yet his accusation had hurt. Tears slowly trickled down my face and neck as my chest constricted and my throat closed up. I was moments away from a total breakdown though I was probably overreacting. He hadn't actually called me a tease, but he didn't say I wasn't one either.

I shook my head. I wasn't going to think about it anymore, I knew if I did that I would breakdown. Pushing all thoughts of Kaelin out of my mind, I instead focused on putting one foot in front of the other. It took me longer than I thought to even reach my backyard though it probably would have taken less time if I didn't have heels on and kept tripping on roots. I was worn out by the time I stepped in my backyard. My legs and back were stiff from sleeping on the ground and hiking in heels.

I crept through my yard momentarily stopping to take off my shoes and continued on my way to my back door. The woods lightened up behind me and illuminated the scene before me, which was my backyard littered with red Solo cups, streamers, and Japanese lanterns that had been torn down.

I didn't really join in the fun and that's how I ended up being with Kaelin. Thinking about him made my chest tighten and feel like I couldn't breathe. I had opened my heart up to let love in, but instead all I got was heartbreak. It was only going to get worse. *Ugh,* I shook myself mentally. I needed to get out of this funk or whatever it was before I fell too far and couldn't get back up. I slunk to my backdoor feeling the dew-covered grass beneath my toes.

I crept up the porch, trying to be as stealthy as I could, and lifted up one of the potted plants beside the door for the spare key. It didn't take me long to find it and unlock the door, opening it as quietly as I could.

"And where have you been, Missy?"

# Chapter 6

I jumped at the sound of her voice though it shouldn't have surprised me that she would be up waiting for me. I turned around to find my mom's dark blue eyes even darker, letting me know she wasn't happy. I gulped. I had expected that she would be cross with me especially since I stayed out all night. I just hoped she didn't find out that I was with Kaelin.

"I-I was just, um, taking a stroll," I replied, not truly lying just telling a half-truth.

Her eyes narrowed as she took in the sight of me. It probably didn't help that I was still in the dress that I had worn last night.

"You were taking a walk all night?" she asked, crossing her arms over her chest.

I chewed on my lower lip as I tried to come up with a better lie, but it was too late. She had caught me.

"I fell asleep in the woods," I admitted, hanging my head. My mom sighed and shook her head, her mocha brown hair swaying.

"Sweetheart, I don't understand why you would be in the woods in the first place." Confusion was written all over her face. *Oh goodness.* I didn't know what to say to that. I couldn't lie to her, yet I couldn't tell her the truth either.

"I, um, just wanted to clear my head." It wasn't quite a lie. I had in fact just wanted to get away from everything though everything didn't seem to include Kaelin.

"Awe, sweetheart, I know you're distraught about the whole Death Call thing, but seeing the death of our first love makes us truly banshees or rather wailing women as some used to call us. It makes us who we are. I know it hurts, but there will be others," she replied, trying to comfort me.

Rising from her chair, she came over and gave me a light hug. Her warmth comforted me, but only for a moment. She was trying to make it better for me, yet it only seemed to make it worse. Now I couldn't stop thinking about Kaelin and the moment we had shared.

I wished I hadn't blown up at him because of a little misunderstanding, though in reality he had known what he had said, there was no misinterpreting it. I pushed those thoughts away. They were only causing me more pain. Pain, I didn't want to deal with at the moment. I smiled halfheartedly.

"How about we bake some cookies," my mom said, walking over to the cabinets plucking out ingredients to make homemade chocolate chip cookies. "Chocolate always helps when you're down."

I smiled for real this time. My mom was the best when it came down to comforting me. She had done the same thing when I was younger when everything seemed to upset me. She would always bake cookies. I loved my mom for that. I mean, yeah, sometimes she could be strict while other times she was the cool mom everyone wished they had.

I helped her set up and fix the mixture for our cookies. As I was rolling a ball of dough and putting it on the tray, I felt something light hit me. I glanced around to find flour floating around me, clinging to my clothes and hair. I glared over at my mother who had a handful of flour, eyes wide with innocence.

"Don't you dare," I warned her, sidling closer to her to collect a handful for myself.

As soon as I scooped up a handful, she threw hers. I turned my head just in time so instead of hitting my face it hit my hair and shoulder. I squealed and threw my handful. It was a full out war. We threw flour all over the place, laughing and giggling, like we were kids again, not mother and daughter.

"Well, I think we used all of the flour," my mom concluded, taking in the mess we had made.

The countertops were covered along with the floor and us. White powder fell like snowflakes, settling on anything in close proximity.

"I guess we have to get more if we want to make more cookies," I decided, studying the pitiful amount of dough we had. We had enough to make maybe half a dozen cookies.

"I think this should be enough for now unless you want to make more," she said, glancing over at me with a smile on her lips.

"Nah, I think we are good." I smiled, chuckling at her flour covered hair and clothes.

It's like we had been out in the snow or a snowstorm with all the flour around us. I brushed my hair out of my face, scattering flour everywhere, and continued to make balls of dough so we could put them in the oven. It didn't take us long to finish. While the cookies were baking, I peeked at my mother's smiling face. She seemed so happy, yet I knew deep down she was just as heartbroken as I soon would be.

"Hey, Mom, was Dad your first love?" I asked softly.

We barely ever talked about my dad. He had died before I was born. I had never questioned it before, but now that I knew the truth about our first Death Call, I had wondered. My mom's body stiffened. Her whole demeanor had changed at the mention of my father. It took her awhile to answer, but when she did, she said softly,

"Yes, we had met in college when I was nineteen. I hadn't fallen for any of my high school classmates so I thought maybe I would never have my first call, but then I met him. It was love at first sight for both of us, and that was when I knew it hadn't forgotten. It was just waiting for me to fall in love," she said sadly. "We had been so young back then that I thought maybe I could change his fate, yet fate never truly changes. It just changes how they die in the end." I strode over to my mom and hugged her sincerely. I had never known. I guess I just didn't want to believe that she had gone through the same pain I was going through now. If my mom had tried to change fate and failed, how was I supposed to do any better? My heart broke into a million pieces as the truth settled in. I couldn't save him . . .

"I'm sorry. I shouldn't have brought it up."

"No, Aislin, you needed to know. I know it will be hard, but the more you fight it the harder it will be to let go. Please, I just don't want you to go through what I did with your father."

I didn't reply. It felt like my world was caving in on me as I struggled to escape the truth. I needed to let him go yet my heart told me to hold on that there had to be a way to save him. It was an internal struggle between my head and my heart. I didn't know which was right.

I pushed all of those thoughts away and tried to concentrate on the present, on the here and now. The smell of cookies wafted through the air, and I was momentarily calmed by it. It made me think of better days when I was younger and only had to deal with mundane things like clothes and dolls. I smiled sadly knowing those days were over now, and I could never bring them back.

Picking up a towel and opening the oven door, I heaved out the tray of golden-brown cookies. They were warm and gooey like they would just melt in my mouth in chocolate goodness. I set the tray down on the counter and glanced back at my mom who seemed to be in worse shape than me.

"Here," I said, picking up a cookie, wincing slightly from the heat, and handed it to her, "chocolate makes everything better."

She smiled, but it didn't reach her eyes. Her blue eyes were cast in shadow, filled with sorrow. I had brought this on her. She used to be so strong, but now she was just a hollow shell filled with memories of a life she could never get back. Was that how I was going to end up, just a hollow shell? Would I feel better if I just gave up? I knew I wouldn't. I wasn't the type to just give up without trying.

I grabbed a cookie, blowing on it for a second and nibbled on it while trying to think of ways that I could somehow change fate, yet if my mom couldn't, how was I supposed to? The struggle started all over again as I fought to find a balance. Even though my mom had failed, I knew I had to try. I couldn't just give up on the only person I had ever loved. If there were any truth to magic and fairytales then love conquers all, even fate. I had to believe that was true or else I would fall into the abyss that was a broken heart.

"Mom, are you going to be all right?" I asked, worry constricting my heart.

I knew that look. I had seen it on Kaydynce's mother's face a week before her tragic departure. The death of a loved one does something to you that makes it hard to live. Mrs. Creek's second husband had died in a car accident, and she hadn't been the same since. She had taken her life soon after in her depression. I didn't want to see my mom go out like that. One loss would be bad, but to lose my mom? That would be even worse.

"Yes, sweetheart, I'll be fine."

I didn't know if I truly believed her. She had that haunted gaze like she was just realizing that her life was finally over. She had finally given up on life. I was beyond worried. I was concerned that she might end it for herself.

"I'm sorry," I said, knowing I was the reason she appeared so lost. If I hadn't brought him up, then we could have still been having fun making cookies.

"It's not your fault, sweetheart. I know you've been wondering about it for a while. I just didn't know how to tell you," she said, trying to hide the longing and sorrow that was left behind from her younger days.

"Mom, was there anybody else? You know, did you ever love another?" I queried, feeling in my heart that I already knew the answer.

"No, your father was the only person I ever truly loved," she said forlornly, "but there is something you should know, Aislin, something many of us still don't know. You may fall for others, but their fate will always be the same. In the end, every Death Call is for someone you have loved fully, with all of your heart."

# Chapter 7

My whole body locked up as I realized what that meant. We are doomed to be alone forever. No matter who or when we fell in love, the ending would still be the same. Death comes for the ones we love. It can't be true, yet I had to take in the evidence. It wasn't an accident that Mrs. Creek's second husband got into a car crash.

It all fit. Both of Mrs. Creek's husbands died meaning it didn't matter if I gave up on Kaelin, in the end I would still be alone. It was my worst fear, but I wasn't going to let it get to me. Life is what we make it. I had to keep on telling myself that until I made myself believe that it was true.

"Is that why you never fell in love again?" I asked cautiously.

My mom was at the breaking point, and I didn't want to push her further. She nodded her head, her hair bobbing with the movement until it just cascaded around her shoulders. Scooting closer to her until our shoulders were touching, she rested her head on my shoulder. We stayed like that for a while until the clock tolled telling us it was eight in the morning. She shook herself and took a deep breath, controlling all of her emotions until she was back to her usual self.

"Well, you better go get changed and ready for practice before you're late," she said, pushing me out of the kitchen.

"All right, all right I'm going." I laughed, jogging to the stairs and up to my room.

It was easy to find what I wanted to wear. It was already lying across my bed like it knew that it was needed. I quickly got dressed, throwing my dress into my hamper, and checked myself in my vanity mirror. My white shorts might be considered a little too short and see through, but no one at school really seemed to care. They showed off my long legs while my pale blue shirt was cut a little low, showing off my bust.

My hair was a different matter to handle. I had sticks, leaves, and flour all through it. I brushed out as much as I could. A few sticks were so tangled in my hair that my brush couldn't even go through it. Sighing in frustration, I yanked out all of the leaves and tried to wrestle with the remaining twigs.

*No wonder Mom knew I was lying.* Throwing my hands up in defeat, I tossed down my brush and left my room. I probably had to cut it out, but I wasn't going to mess with it now. As I was shuffling down the stairs, I remembered that I had forgotten my gym bag. I rushed back upstairs and into my room and grabbed my blue and white bag. I slung it over my shoulder and sauntered down the stairs again.

"Bye, Mom. I'll be back in a couple hours," I called, walking out the door.

The day was warm and sunny with a slight breeze that ruffled my hair. I scanned the sky, feeling the sun warm my skin, and watched as a few clouds strolled by. I strolled to my car and noticed a yellow sticky note stuck to my windshield. I peeled it off and read it slowly as a smile spread across my lips.

**Aislin,**

**I'm sorry about what I said. I didn't mean it like that. It just seems surreal that someone as beautiful as you would**

like a guy like me. I just want to make it up to you. How about I take you out on a date, and we can see how it goes? If it goes badly then I'll let you be. I just want a chance, please.

**Kaelin**

I stuffed the note into my pocket, got into my burgundy Ford Fiesta, and headed to school for track practice. The school was only fifteen minutes away from my house, so it didn't take me long to get there. I pulled up just as Teagan was getting out of her blue Cavalier. She wore plain pink T-shirt and black Bermuda shorts. She had also put her wavy black hair into a high ponytail that fell just below her shoulder blades.

"Hey," I called out, getting out of my car.

She turned and smiled, her hair swinging behind her.

"Hey, Aislin," she said, walking over to me.

Her smile was contagious causing me to smile back at her. It had been a while since I had seen that smile come out. She used to smile all the time before Cole's death. I was glad to see her smiling again yet deep down I was worried especially after what my mom had divulged. I didn't want to see Teagan get hurt again. I didn't want to see any of us getting hurt, but there was nothing I could do to stop it. All I could do was soften the blow.

"Why are you all smiles and sunshine?" I asked, nudging her shoulder lightly.

Her pale cheeks turned a faint pink, the color of the sky during a sunrise. Her pale green eyes shone brightly with pure joy and a hint of hope. My heart broke as I gazed at her shimmering body. Pure, innocent happiness radiated from her face. I couldn't shatter what little happiness Teagan had left. I couldn't be that heartless though I could stop this here and now, so she didn't have to go through the same heartache as before. I couldn't bring myself to do it though. Maybe Mom was wrong, and that Mrs. Creek's husbands' deaths were just a coincidence.

"Well, I met someone. Actually, we've been seeing each other for a while, but we finally made it official," she squealed, reminding me of Kaydynce and how she always squealed when she was happy or excited.

I was happy yet melancholy for her as I thought about what would happen if this new guy wound up dead and how she would react. I wanted to push these thoughts away, but I knew I had to ask her. I needed to know what the repercussions would be. Teagan was the sensible one out of the group. She always kept us from getting into big trouble whenever Kaydynce persuaded us to do something dangerous or reckless.

I smiled sadly. "I'm happy for you, Teagan."
"But?"
"But what?" I asked, feigning ignorance.

"You know what, Aislin, so spill it. What's the but?" she asked, crossing her arms over her chest and glared at me like a mother catching her child lying.
"It's just . . . you have been through so much, and I just don't want to see you hurt again," I confided, peeking up at her.
"I know. I have the same doubts, but I'm sick of feeling sorry for myself. I want to feel love and passion again. I'm sick

of being the uptight, strict one while you and Kaydynce run around having fun. I know it's not like that, but I want to feel complete again no matter how short it will be. I know the consequences, but I just want to live again. I'm tired of feeling heartbroken."

She gazed down at me, her eyes pleading me to just let it go and try to be happy for her. Yet I didn't know if I could be happy for her when I knew what would happen if it ended badly, but I sucked it up and pretended that everything would be fine.

"So, who is this lucky guy?" I asked, actually curious as we ambled to the dirt track that circled the football field.

"Aaron McCloud. I know, I didn't think it would happen, but I was at the mall one day and noticed him. I sauntered over to him, and we just started talking. We actually have a lot in common like we both love to run and enjoy just strolling through the woods," she said excitedly like she couldn't contain her joy anymore.

I was glad to see this side of Teagan again though I knew it would be short lived. I tried to think back on who Aaron was. The name sounded familiar then it hit me. Aaron had been Kaelin's best friend before he moved. They were complete opposites. Aaron was the shy, keep-to-himself guy while Kaelin was the outgoing, partying, friendly guy. Though their personalities were different, they fit together like strawberries and chocolate.

Weird analogy, but hey it works. Aaron used to be the loner type until he met Kaelin, the guy who could bring anybody out of his or her shell. After Kaelin left though, Aaron fell back into the loner scene. It was sad really. I guess losing the only friend you had would do that to a person.

I remembered his sandy-blond hair and baby blue eyes that were always hidden behind his green-rimmed glasses. He hadn't been bad looking. He was actually kind of cute with his boyish appearance though the glasses kind of detracted from it a little. He was a sweet guy, someone I could see Teagan falling for, and that was the problem. I frowned, thinking that maybe I should tell her. It would hopefully take away some of the inevitable pain that would soon follow if I was right about how her feelings worked.

Yet when I opened my mouth to tell her, no words came out, and I was left like a fish out of water. My heart constricted. I didn't know if I would be saving her pain or making it worse. Teagan's green eyes scrutinized me... Yet no matter how hard I tried, the words wouldn't come out. It was like my tongue was made of lead. I shook my head, maybe it was best if I didn't tell her just in case my mom had been wrong. I didn't want to give her false information or false hope, but that was just what I was giving her by not ending this right here and now.

Yet there was one truth that I needed to know before things got any worse. I hoped my gut feeling was wrong, but it had never steered me astray. I hoped it was mistaken. "Teagan," I whispered, taking her aside so that I could talk to her privately without the prying eyes of our track mates, "are you in love with him?"

Fearing what she would say, I knew the answer just from the expression in her eyes. I hung my head in despair as my mom's words played through my head. *In the end every Death Call is for someone you have loved fully, with all of your heart . . .*

"Aislin, I know it's wrong especially since I-I loved Cole but I can't help what I feel. I'm in love with Aaron. He has my heart" *With all of your heart. He is going to die, and I'm powerless to save him. Teagan hasn't a clue what she has done.*

# Chapter 8

Closing my eyes, a pressure built in my head as I tried to think of a way to save them both. I couldn't fault her though. I was in the same boat. I knew Kaelin's death was near, yet she didn't know anything about Aaron's. I didn't know what to do, and it was getting harder and harder to think as the pressure in my head intensified. Someone or something banged on the inside trying to get out.

"Come on," I said, towing her toward the track, "we need to start running before coach catches us slacking off."

She nodded in agreement, and the conversation ended there. We ran in silence. Jogging used to calm my thoughts and make me feel peaceful, but not today. Instead of feeling at ease, I felt restless like when I can't sleep so I toss and turn all night. It felt like there was something I should do or remember yet I couldn't put my finger on it.

I shook it off like raindrops, pretending or rather ignoring the irrational feeling not thinking anything of it. I pushed all of my thoughts away and just tried to concentrate on moving my legs to feel the burn that came with running. It was a good kind of pain one that always made me push myself harder. I egged myself on, pushing myself further until I passed Teagan and a few of my track mates. It was exhilarating to just focus on my running instead of all of the things that were clouding my mind.

As I ran, I remembered what I had forgotten or needed to do. I forgot I had left Kaydynce in the woods after her little incident last night. She must have found her way home yet what if she didn't? I would have that on my conscience if I were wrong. I had to tell myself that she was safe at home just sleeping off all of the essences she had taken last night. I slowed down my pace so Teagan could catch up with me.

"Hey, Teagan, did you see Kaydynce leave last night?" I asked, feeling a sense of foreboding.

"No, actually I didn't, and she wasn't at practice either. I heard they had to cancel cheerleading practice because both she and her co-captain were absent." Uh oh. Kaydynce never missed a practice unless it was very important. I couldn't think the worst. Maybe she was just sick or sleeping off the essence hangover.

"That's weird. I hope she made it home safely last night," I said, worry clouding my mind. Guilt also took a ride on my thoughts. I had left her...

"I bet she did, Aislin, don't worry. She will be fine. She is tough and can handle anything," she replied, slowing down and wrapped an arm around my shoulder in comfort.

"I know she is, but she is like the little sister I never had. I worry about her especially since lately she has been having problems controlling her hunger." Teagan frowned

"What do you mean she has been having problems controlling her hunger?" she asked, with a hint of something I couldn't identify in her voice.

"Well last night she almost drained a guy. She would have if I hadn't found her and stopped her. She looked like a person on crack needing a fix. It was something I hadn't seen in her, not after she learned how to control it."

"That really isn't like her. Well hopefully she is just resting at home," Teagan said half-heartedly.

She had better be at home sleeping because the other alternative wasn't good. Kaydynce had only lost control once when she first started experiencing the "hunger" her first year of high school. It was also the day that I admitted to myself that I had feelings for Kaelin, and also the day he left.

*"Aislin. Aislin, wake up," Kaydynce yelled, shaking me awake.*

*"What?" I asked groggily. I didn't particularly like being woken up especially when I was having an amazing dream about being out on a date with Channing Tatum, and he was reciting poetry for me while giving me a wonderful back massage. It was the perfect dream, yet Kaydynce had to go and ruin it.*

*"You've over slept. We're late for school."*

*"What?" I yelled, jumping out of my bed and scrambling around for clothes to wear then I heard pearly laughter.*

*I turned around and gave Kaydynce one of my death glares.*

*"It's Saturday, silly. I just wanted to see what you would do, Miss always on time," she teased, tossing herself onto my bed.*

*Her blond hair bobbed around her face as she settled into my covers. Picking up one of my pillows, I threw it at her.*

*"Get out of my bed, Kaydynce, and tell me why you woke me up at—" I gazed at the clock on my nightstand. "—eight o'clock in the morning," I said, stifling a yawn.*

*She turned on her stomach and rested her head on her hands with her elbows up mischief playing behind her blue eyes. She had on a pair of daisy duke shorts and a mid-drift pink shirt that read, "Bite me." Her lips were glossed a bright pink while her eyes were heavily laden with eyeliner.*

*"Well, I thought it would be fun to have like a girl's day out or something. School has been taking away all of the fun, and I thought high school was supposed to be fun."*

*"I think you are thinking about college, Kay, anyways it's not my fault that you don't do your homework or pay attention in class. If you did you might actually learn something." She brushed it off, waving her hand in the air.*

*"Nevertheless, Teagan is waiting downstairs for us, so you better hurry up and get dressed," she said, running away as I tried to swat at her.*

*She knew I didn't like being bossed around so she does it anyway. I sighed. This was going to be a long and troublesome day. It always was with Kaydynce around. At least with Teagan here she could possibly prevent the many disasters that followed Kaydynce wherever she went.*

*I rummaged through my closest trying to find something cute to wear. After a couple of minutes, I settled on a pair of tight, black skinny jeans and a purple peasant blouse that was ruffled around the sleeves so I could hang them off my shoulders. I put on a dash of makeup: eyeliner, purple eye shadow, and pink lip-gloss.*

*Walking down the stairs, I was greeted by two grinning faces, which meant trouble was soon to follow. Teagan was wearing a plaid skirt, knee-high socks, a button up top, and her hair in pigtails. She was all decked out, which only meant we were going boy hunting.*

*"All right, Teagan, Kaydynce, where are we going?" I asked, meeting them at the bottom of the stairs. They both giggled, exchanging looks.*

*Screaming at the same time, "We're going to the mall!" I glared at them.*

*"What's the catch?" I asked, studying them.*

*Exchanging gazes again, they didn't say anything. I sighed. I wasn't going to get an answer until we got there. They got on either side of me and locked arms then we were out the door. Teagan's car was parked out front, and we all piled in. The drive to the mall didn't take us long at all, but the whole time I was trying to decipher what they had in store for me. I knew it couldn't be good. Both Teagan and Kaydynce were the mischievous type meaning they always got into trouble though Teagan usually stopped us before going too far. I just hoped today was going to be one of those days and not the ones where Kaydynce went over the edge, bringing us with her.*

*Teagan pulled into a parking lot, and we all got out, adjusting our outfits so that we would look our best. The sun bore down on us, yet nothing could faze us at this point as we sauntered to the entranceway. We were three hot girls strutting into the mall hoping for something or someone to catch our eyes. As we marched, I noticed a stand to the right of us. It read "Kissing Booth". I glared at it for a moment until I discerned that it was getting closer. I glanced at Teagan and Kaydynce's faces. Both were grinning like fools.*

*"Please tell me this isn't why we are at the mall at nine o' clock in the morning," I groaned, knowing that this was exactly why we were here. Teagan and Kaydynce had set up a kissing booth to attract boys. Don't get me wrong it would work it just seemed so wrong.*

*"Teagan, you're up first," Kaydynce said, pushing Teagan into the booth where a small line had formed.*

*Teagan and Kaydynce had set up the booth for five dollars a kiss, and guys were falling all over it just to kiss one of us. It was amusing at first as all the boys gathered in a line and fidgeted, waiting for their turn. It didn't matter what they looked like or if they were popular each boy got a turn though the ones, we thought were cute got our numbers.*

*Everything was going smoothly until Kaelin showed up, and then all hell broke loose as Kaydynce tried to gain his attention. Kaelin and I had been friends since grade school. We were inseparable, as two best friends usually were but today seemed different.*

*There was a new aura about him like something had changed yet didn't if you can believe that. He was wearing a navy blue polo, cargo pants, and his hair was ruffled like he had just gotten out of bed. My heart skipped a beat when he smiled at me. His smile lit up the room, or rather area, like the sun had just hit its peak at noon.*

*I smiled back, warmth spreading up my body. We continued to smile at each other, but then it was over as Kaydynce butted in.*

*"Kaelin!" she squealed, jumping from one foot to the other.*

*All of the guys looked to see who had caught her attention. Kaelin just waved, seeming a little self-conscious, which was weird for Mr. Popular. Something really was different about him, yet I couldn't figure out what. I raised a brow. He just shrugged his shoulders like it was nothing. I shrugged it off too thinking maybe I was just seeing things.*

*"So, who's next?" Kaydynce called, as she took her place as the main attraction at the kissing booth.*

*Every hand shot up except Kaelin's at her call. I frowned.* Maybe he wants to kiss Teagan instead, *but an inner voice said another. I shook my head. He couldn't be here for me, or could he? I didn't want to think of the possibility. It might jeopardize our friendship. I had to shake off this feeling. There was no way he was here for me. It wasn't possible. As I was worrying about whether or not Kaelin was here for me, Kaydynce's posture changed and so did the atmosphere around us.*

*Glancing up just in time, I saw Kaydynce start to suck the life from an unsuspecting boy. Kaydynce's hunger had just begun. I looked toward Teagan for help, and she shook her head at me. She didn't know what to do either. Fear gripped me as I watched her slowly drain the boy's essence. I had to do something. I pushed her away with my hip, breaking the connection momentarily.*

*"Wow," the boy murmured, as he stumbled away from the booth.*

*I let out a sigh of relief, but the danger wasn't over yet. Kaelin's turn had finally come, and it was probably the worst timing ever.*

*"Hey, Kaelin, um, this probably isn't a good time. You should probably go. Actually, all of you should go. The kissing booth is done for today," I called out, hoping it would send away most of the boys. I heard groans and complaints, but everyone was leaving except the one person I wanted as far away from Kaydynce as possible, Kaelin.*

*"I'm not leaving, Aislin, I really need to talk to you," he looked around and whispered, "in private."*

*My heartbeat sped up again, but this time in excitement not in fear. Yet like anything good in my life, it was ruined. Without a single warning, Kaydynce pushed me out of the way and grabbed Kaelin, kissing him deeply. He struggled until her hunger kicked in again, stealing his essence.*

*"Kaydynce, stop before you kill him!" I screamed.*

*I caught Teagan's eyes, pleading for help. She shook her head, pity written all over her face. Growling in frustration, I charged at Kaydynce hoping to dislodge her. She sidestepped me. Fear clogged my throat as time slowly ticked away along with his life. Just as I ran out of ideas, so did his life. She let go of him, licking her lips with a Cheshire grin plastered there.*

*"Noooo!" I cried, jumping out of the kissing entrance to catch him before he hit the floor.*

*"Teagan, help me carry him to—" I glanced around for a private place. "—over there," I said, pointing at an open door which led to the janitor's closet. She nodded, rushing over to me and grabbed one of his arms slinging it over her shoulder. I did the same, and we both shuffled to the open door. No one seemed to notice or care that a boy had just died.*

*"What about Kaydynce?" Teagan asked, peeking over her shoulder at the hunger-filled Kaydynce.*

*"We are going to need her help, and we need it quickly," I said, my heart constricting as Kaelin's body slowly grew colder.*

*We made it to the room and set him down on the floor. I nodded toward Kaydynce. Teagan nodded in understanding and went off to collect her. I bit my lower lip. I hoped it would work. I had never seen it performed, but I knew it could be done. Kaydynce had the ability to bring him back, but I didn't know if she had learned the ability yet. She was young and just getting her powers. Teagan hauled in a struggling Kaydynce and closed the door, locking it.*

*"Kaydynce," I said, slapping her once to make her focus, "We need your help. We need you to breathe life into Kaelin."*

*Kaydynce's brows furrowed for a moment then she saw the still body on the floor. Her skin became ashen. She began to shake.*

*"I-I d-didn't mean to, I swear, Aislin," she stuttered, tears collecting in the corner of her eyes.*

*"I know, Kay," I uttered, slinging my arm around her. "But I need you to bring him back now. You remember when we saw that show, about a succubus?" she nodded, as a few tears trickled down her cheeks, "well you remember how she could kill someone then breathe life into them again? Well, that's what I need you to do right now."*

*She sniffled and then leaned down breathing into Kaelin's mouth. At first nothing happened.*

*"It's okay, Kay, you can do it. I believe in you."*

*Taking a deep breath, she tried again this time wisps of blue poured back into him. I smiled in relief as he took his first breath. I hugged Kaydynce, thankful that I hadn't been wrong or rather that the TV show hadn't or else we would have a dead body on our hands. Kaelin opened his eyes and looked around at all of us groggily. He smiled one of his cocky grins as he took in all three of us leaning over him.*

*"Well, I must have gotten pretty lucky to have all three of y'all in a room and not remember what happened," he said, his honey colored eyes twinkling. I smiled shaking my head.*

*"Yeah, you got pretty lucky, Kaelin," I said, though I hadn't been joking. I was just glad that I had him back.*

*"Oh, didn't you want to tell me something?" I asked just remembering that he had said something about needing to talk.*

"*Yeah, hey Kaydynce and Teagan can y'all leave us alone for a moment, please.*"

*They both giggled, but eventually they left, leaving us completely alone. Kaelin sat up so that we were gazing at each other, and for some reason I just wanted to lean in and fill the space between us. I resisted the urge and instead stayed perfectly still and waited for Kaelin to speak. He reached a hand out slowly and tucked away a stray hair behind my ear. My eyes closed as the feel of his fingers lightly brushed my cheek.*

"*Aislin . . .*" *he said, his breath light against my face.*

*I opened my eyes slowly only to lose myself in his. He was mere inches away from me. I wanted to back up slowly yet at the same time I wanted to be even closer.*

"*Yes?*" *I whispered, not wanting to break the moment.*

*As I stared into his eyes, I saw sadness and longing, yet I didn't know which one would win out. I felt his fingers brush against my cheek again then his hand cupped my cheek. I leaned into it closing my eyes again. His touch made my skin heat up, and all I wanted to do was feel more.*

"*I'm leaving,*" *he whispered back.*

*My eyes snapped open, and I pushed away from him.*

"*What? When? Why?*" *Panic grabbed ahold of me again.*

"*Yeah, I'm going to go live with my mom for a while. I can't handle my dad anymore especially since he got a new girlfriend.*" *He rubbed the back of his head, looking away.* "*Anyways, I'm actually leaving tonight. I just wanted to say goodbye before I left.*"

*He couldn't leave...not yet.*

*"Can't you stay with one of your friends? I bet one of them would let you stay with them for a while," I said, trying in vain to find a way for him to stay.*

*"I couldn't do that to them plus I'll be back. I just need some time away, but I will be back, Aislin, I promise you," he said, heaving me into a tight hug.*

*Tears stream down my cheeks as I thought of all of the good times we had together, and now we wouldn't have anymore because he was leaving. He let me cry into his shoulder. One of his hands caressed my hair. This was it...*

"Aislin, come on before we have to run even more laps," Teagan said, dragging me behind her as she started to run. I snapped out of my reminiscing and pushed myself to keep up with Teagan, whom was running for dear life.

"Why are we in such a hurry, Teagan?" I asked, running beside her.

"We are the last ones, so if we don't finish now then the whole team will kick our asses since we are the fastest," she said, exasperated.

"True." I pushed myself even harder until we both crossed the finish line.

"I'm glad you two could join us," Mrs. Jones yelled, blowing her whistle, "Practice is over." Everyone sighed in relief though a few gave us the evil eye.

Teagan and I skipped to our cars glad practice was over, but we were still worried about Kaydynce.

"Hey, how about we take my car and see if she is home," I said, hoping that she was at home and not somewhere else.

I had a bad feeling we weren't going to find her, but I pushed that feeling down and got into my car. Teagan got into the passenger seat, and we were off in search of Kaydynce.

"Do you think her hunger is finally winning out again?" Teagan asked, frowning up at the sky.

"I hope not or else we're all screwed," I replied.

We drove in silence after that, both of us musing over the possible places she could be if not at home. We pulled up into her driveway, and I automatically noticed that her silver mustang wasn't in the driveway. *That's a bad sign.* We got out and walked up her wooden porch to the door. I rapped on it lightly and heard tiny footsteps shuffle to the door.

"How may I help you, young ladies?" Ms. Crain, Kaydynce's grandma, asked as she opened the door.

"We're wondering if Kaydynce is home," I replied, smiling sweetly.

"I'm sorry, dear, but I haven't seen her since she left for your party." Our worst fears were put into motion.

Kaydynce was missing.

# Chapter 9

I glanced at Teagan hoping she had a plan on how we were going to find Kaydynce. She could be anywhere. I couldn't think of where she would go, but I figured it would be somewhere either very populated or secluded. The possibilities were immense. There were so many places she could go. Teagan frowned.

"Where was the last place you saw her, Aislin?"

I thought about it for a moment. Where had I left her? Right!

"The last place I saw her was in the woods. I had just stopped her from draining some guy, and she had passed out, so I set her against a tree," I said.

Teagan smiled, hope rising as we both set out again to find our missing succubus.

"Do you think she would still be there?"

"I don't know, Teagan, but at least we know she was there so maybe we can find a sign of where she went next," I said, fidgeting in my seat as worry and fear set in.

Worry for where she was and fear of what she was doing. My fear won over my worry as I thought back on the many times Kaydynce had lost control, causing havoc all over. In all of the times Kaydynce had lost control, she had only killed two people. I just hoped it stayed at only two and nothing more. A sense of foreboding wrapped itself around me.

We drove in silence once again as we both checked out the windows for any obvious signs of Kaydynce being there. We pulled up into my driveway, and both jumped out. Thankfully my mom was busy with planning another party to notice our sudden intrusion.

We dashed into the forest searching for any marks that Kaydynce had been there. There were a few broken branches and scuffed up dirt, but that could have been from Kaelin and me running through it. So far there wasn't a clue, but we weren't going to give up.

As we searched, I felt a tingling in my throat again and a buzzing in my head. I turned to look over at Teagan and found her frozen to the spot. Her face had paled, and her eyes were wide. I turned my gaze toward where she was staring. I gulped, heart galloping in my ears.

The wraith had come back, and it didn't appear happy to see me. Its black form withered and twisted. It's face stayed hidden. The woods darkened around us even though the sun had barely reached its peak. The wraith seemed to have absorbed all of the light, leaving us in darkness.

Fear clawed at my throat trying to break free as my knees buckled under me again. I shook my head in denial. I knew what was coming next. I didn't want to believe it would happen again. I wasn't ready to see Kaelin's fate changed by my actions...again. Chills went down my spine as the wraith's empty eye sockets bore into my soul, ripping out my banshee cry. My scream echoed through the woods. I wasn't the only one experiencing the Death Call.

I had just enough time to see Teagan fall to her knees and tilt her head back letting out her own banshee cry. My eyes blurred with unshed tears as the new vision invaded my mind.

"Hey, Kaydynce, have you seen Aislin? I need to talk to her about something," Kaelin asked, as she and someone else passed by him.

"I haven't a clue, Kae, but I'm sure we can find her," she said lightly, caressing his arm.

She sauntered away, letting her fingers slowly slip off his arm to lie by her side. He soon followed her in a trance. Kaydynce had used her power of persuasion to take away Kaelin's will along with another guy. All three left with Kaydynce in front, and the boys following close behind.

Kaydynce wore the same outfit she had to my party: a tight, strapless pink dress that showed off all of her curves. Her eyes glowed a bright blue as her hunger pushed to be appeased. She glanced back at the boys and licked her lips as a grin spread across her face. She cringed, scrunching up her face. Kaydynce clutched her stomach, her eyes brightening even more.

Kaydynce led them to a deserted dirt road with only a few tire marks, which were covered by dead leaves. Maples, oaks, elms, and hickory trees lined the outside with an assortment of colored leaves scattered everywhere. The road was only a few minutes away from the high school.

Sweat pooled on the boys' brows with the heat intensifying as they continued to walk. The sun cast a shadow across the path, but a few rays escaped peeking through the branches. Kaydynce turned around suddenly, stopping the boys in their tracks, and smiled with a glint in her glowing eyes. Shaking his head, Kaelin snapped out of Kaydynce's trance.

"Where are we and where is Aislin?" Kaelin asked.

He looked around at the long forgotten road, fear spreading through as the light dimmed even more. He shivered and glanced *at Kaydynce. Her whole body glowed a pale blue matching her eyes. He wasn't the only one full of fear. The other guy backed away from her, his eyes turning to saucers. Kaydynce's smile widened as she noticed him backing away. She strode over to him, touching his arm lightly. His body at once relaxed and sagged a little.*

*"You can do so much better than her, Kaelin," she purred, stroking the boy's arm and turned to Kaelin. "I'm better than her!" she snapped.*

*Her hand clenched around the other guy's arm as her eyes flashed. Kaelin took a step toward her then paused, eyes shifting from her to the other guy then back again. The boy whimpered as she put more pressure on his arm.*

*"Calm down. Let's talk about this, Kay," Kaelin said, taking cautious steps toward her with his hands raised.*

*"No! I will **not** calm down! I deserve love just as much as Aislin and Teagan!" she protested. "If I can't be loved then they shouldn't be either!" she screeched, her eyes glowing even brighter.*

*She yanked the boy closer to herself and laid her lips on his. The moment their lips touched, she started to suck the life out of him. His pale blue essence flowed into Kaydynce's body, appeasing her hunger for a bit. She threw the body down, licking her lips then made eye contact with Kaelin. Kaelin shivered, his breath quickening at the sight he had just seen.*

*"What are you?" he whispered.*

*He backed up, looking from her glowing body to the still form beside her foot. She kicked the body and sauntered toward Kaelin with a smile of absolute glee.*

*"You won't have to worry about that after I'm done with you,"* *she said, catching his arm as he backed away.*

*Kaelin's body slumped as all of the tension left, leaving him completely vulnerable. Kaydynce's smile widened as she ran her hand up his bicep to his cheek.*

*"I'm going to enjoy this," she whispered.*

*Kaydynce leaned in and lightly brushed her lips against his then slowly stole his soul. She took her time, running her hands all over his sculpted abs and biceps. She pressed her body up against him and felt his heart stutter as she drained the last drop of his spirit.*

Tears streamed down my cheeks as I pounded on the ground with both of my fists. I didn't know which hurt worse that I saw Kaelin die or that Kaydynce had been the one to do it. Every vision brought more pain to my constantly broken heart. I looked up through blurry eyes at the bright sun that shone above us, lighting our way. I wiped away my tears, pushing myself up and searched for Teagan.

She was huddled up beside me, her black hair splayed out around her, with an expression of horror in her big green eyes. Her whole body shook. I ran over to her and cradled her in my arms, rocking back and forth. I had never seen Teagan so out of control. Her body shuddered as she let it all out. Her tears soaked my shirt, but I didn't mind.

"Teagan, what happened?" I asked, frowning.

"I-I saw . . . I-I saw his . . . death. I saw Aaron's death," she whispered.

# Chapter 10

My whole body stiffened. Could it be possible? Did it really happen? I kept on asking myself. It seemed impossible. But Teagan wouldn't lie, and I knew what I saw. Somehow, we both had a Death Call though mine kept on changing. Could it have been because of the wraith? Thinking back on it Teagan was the first to see it, yet it had stared at me. I shook my head. I couldn't think about this right now. I had more pressing matters to deal with like saving Kaelin's soul from being drained.

"Teagan, sweetheart, I need you to get up and be strong. We need to hurry before we're too late," I said.

There were a few clouds blocking the sun, but I knew if we didn't hurry now before the sun reached its peak then we wouldn't be able to save either of them. The woods were still silent around us like it was holding its breath, waiting for us to make our move. The forest had a dangerous feel like a predator was in our midst creating absolute silence. It was like the world around us was frozen in time.

I could only guess that Aaron was the other guy Kaydynce had led to his doom on the deserted road. Teagan was still shaking like a leaf as I pushed her up and off me. Her green eyes were wide and glazed over. It was like she was gazing through me and into the near future. I stood and wrapped one arm around her waist, steadying her shivering body. She rested her head on my shoulder as I drew her forward.

"I know where she is. She is going to Broken Creek Road. I just hope we make it in time," I whispered, as we scrambled back to my car.

The sun was steadily rising as my words fell on deaf ears. Driving to our destination wasn't any better. Silence engulfed us like an ominous fog settling over a city. It felt like the drive to our target was never ending when in fact it only took three minutes. We jumped out of my car as soon as it stopped. Teagan had regained her composure, but I didn't know how long it would last.

We raced through the dusty road, avoiding branches that reached out and tried to grab us and roots that strained to trip us up. The woods had grown up, spreading across the deserted path. Yet it seemed like the forest was encroaching on us as we made a mad dash to save our guys. As the vegetation crept on us, the road stretched on, the more we ran the farther away our goal seemed. I still hadn't caught sight of any of them. Had I been mistaken? Was there another decrepit path that I had forgotten about?

I shook my head, pushing those thoughts away. I knew I hadn't been wrong. Our presence and another were affecting the woods. Magic was in the air and a certain succubus was using her powers on the environment around us. Depending on the type of being, different things come to life that humans would never notice whenever a supernatural being was around.

If a vampire roamed around, the woods would fall silent, and everything would still. Yet if a fairy fluttered around, the forest would rejoice and bustle with noise, as it would bring happiness and peace to nature. Certain beings caused certain reactions in the wildlife, for instance being a banshee makes nature want to comfort as we are continuously filled with sorrow.

Yet what Kaydynce was doing was using her succubus powers to control the vegetation like a wood nymph would, except she wasn't using it for good. Her powers had taken a dark turn causing everything around her to become, well frankly, evil. At the slightest touch, she could make the trees, and other plants bend to her will doing whatever she wanted. It was a scary thought to think about. She could control anything or anyone just by the slightest touch.

"Aislin, is it just me or are we getting nowhere?" Teagan asked.

She glanced over at me with her brow furrowed and a frown on her red lips.

"We will make it. We just have to run faster. It's only Kaydynce playing tricks on our minds. It's just an illusion," I said, pushing myself harder and willing myself to believe that it was true, that it was only an illusion.

"I don't like this feeling, Aislin. It feels like we are going into the lion's den without any protection."

Her voice shook while her eyes held all the fear in the world as we trudged on. I couldn't soothe her fears as my own settled in. Finally, they came into view. We had made it just in time or so I had thought.

"Kaydynce, stop! Don't do this!" I yelled, as Kaydynce grabbed Aaron and held him close.

Teagan dashed passed me, her long black hair swaying behind her, and body slammed into Kaydynce's. Taking Aaron with them, they fell to the ground their breaths whooshing out of their bodies as they made contact. Kaelin was the first to reach him. He caught him just before he touched the earth. I rushed over to them and knelt beside Kaelin. He shook Aaron's body.

"Aaron, buddy, wake up!" Kaelin shook him more then looked over at me. "What's wrong with him? Why isn't he waking up?" Kaelin asked.

He held my gaze, searching for the answers that I could never tell him. I avoided his golden stare and instead concentrated on checking for a pulse. I tested his wrist first, hoping for at least a weak pulse, there wasn't any. Next, I checked his neck, but I couldn't find a pulse at all. I studied the poor boy.

He had barely lived when death took him. His body was slowly showing signs of post mortem: cold skin, blue hue to his lips, and dead eyes. Death came in swift, taking away all of his warmth. Hands grabbed my shoulders and shook me lightly.

"Aislin, tell me, what's wrong with Aaron?"
"He's dead." No point in lying.

He let go of my shoulders like he had been electrocuted and stared at me with wide, unbelieving eyes. Teagan met my gaze with tears streaming down her face. She turned away from me and lifted Kaydynce up to just slam her down again.

"You bitch! How could you.? Bring him back, damn it! I know you can!" Teagan screamed, slamming Kaydynce's body continuously.

Kaydynce only smiled, her eyes shone with pure evil. She had become a monster in our eyes in less than a day. Blood leaked from her lips.

"Oh, boohoo, poor Teagan all alone again. It's so sad... Not! I am so sick and tired of hearing about your boyfriends and how great they are. Neither of you deserve them." She looked pass Teagan and glared at me, "Especially you, Aislin, you don't deserve him. He should have been mine!"

"Kaydynce, you will find love eventually, but right now I need you to bring Aaron back, and we can forget that any of this ever happened."

"No, but you know what I will do," she said, with an evil grin, "I'll drain her instead."

She tugged Teagan close and latched her lips on hers. Teagan struggled, but Kaydynce was too strong. Blue tendrils spread across Teagan's arms and then to Kaydynce's lips. I leapt up and ran over to them, wrapping my arms around Teagan's waist and wrenched them apart. Teagan crumbled in my arms, all of her energy gone. We both fell to the floor from the impact. I checked her pulse, hoping I didn't lose her too. My body relaxed. She was still breathing.

"You ruin everything!" Kaydynce screamed, picking herself up off the ground.

She stomped her feet and crossed her arms like a little kid having a tantrum. Her blond hair was disheveled, and her dress was torn from the fall.

"I'll get my revenge. You'll see!" she yelled, before vanishing into a cloud of smoke.

*How the hell did she do that?* I asked myself but shook the thought away. I didn't really want to know plus I had other things to worry about than Kaydynce's magic trick. I cradled Teagan in my arms, brushing back stray hairs that had come loose of her ponytail.

She seemed so peaceful in her sleep. I wished I could give her that peace, but our lives were only filled with sorrow. I heard his shuffling footsteps before his body heat engulfed me.

"What the hell is going on here, Aislin?" he asked.

I could feel his glare even before I saw it. It bore into the back of my head.

"Can we talk about this later, Kaelin? It's been hard on me too."

"No, Damn it. My best friend is dead, and it's somehow because of Kaydynce. I want to know what the hell is going on, and how the hell she did this."

He flung his arms around emphasizing what he meant. I closed my eyes, trying my hardest to not break down and tell him the truth.

"Kaelin, I-I can't, not here and not now at least, later though, I promise."

"You know what, Aislin. You can keep your damn promise. I'll find out on my own," he said, squaring his shoulders as he turned and paced away from me.

My shoulders slumped. I felt like the weight of the world was on my shoulders, and there wasn't a way to relieve the pressure. I had an unconscious Teagan in my arms, a dead body a few feet away, an evil succubus who wanted Kaelin, and to top it all off Kaelin was trying to uncover everything that we had tried to hide for centuries. What else could go wrong?

# Chapter 11

Weeks went by since the incident with Kaydynce. I tried to pretend that she hadn't killed a boy or that she hadn't tried to drain Teagan of her soul. It was hard to think of the little blond girl I had known who loved to play with her dolls was now a teenager out to get revenge on the people she thought had wronged her.

I couldn't fathom why she had been so keen on destroying the ones Teagan and I loved. It was harder on Teagan though especially. The police had come and gotten our statements...heart attack was the verdict. It didn't sit well for either of us, but it was better than the usual animal attack our kind would say.

I sighed. Neither of us could understand why Kaydynce was acting this way, but I knew if we didn't stop her now, then there would be a lot more bodies for the police to find. The world around us seemed to keep on moving even though one of our classmate's life had ended. It was like a bad dream in which everyone thought they would wake up from yet this wasn't a dream, this was my reality.

I could never wake up from the deaths and sorrows that were soon to come. Teagan's life would never be the same, and it scared me. There was no telling what was going through her mind. I hoped she could make it through, but that's asking a lot out of her. I shook my head, pushing away every other thought except school as I walked down the deserted hallway.

My thoughts had distracted me from hearing the tolling of the bell for class to start. I was late, but I wasn't the only one.

There was another student hanging by one of the many lockers or at least I thought she was a student. When I got closer to her, I noticed that I didn't recognize her. She also didn't look like a teenager, more like a young adult. She had long, glossy black hair that fell down to her waist. She must have sensed me approaching her because she turned around suddenly and locked eyes with me.

Her eyes were a smoky blue or gray like cloudy water or storm clouds. She was wearing a white pants suit though at a distance it looked like normal clothes. Her lips were set into a frown like something was bothering her.

"Can I help you?" I asked, as I took a few more steps closer.

She cocked her head to the side. Her eyes studying me then she smiled.

"I am Celestial Brook, and I am seeking Kaydynce Creek though if you are who I presume you are then yes you can help me by pointing me in the direction of where she might be."

"Um, down the hall, and it's the door on the right, but may I ask why you are looking for her."

"That is none of your concern, but I thank you for your cooperation," she said.

She gave a bow and strode off toward the door I had pointed out to her. *Hmmm, that was weird and a tad bit suspicious,* I thought as I scampered toward my first class. As soon as I entered my classroom, all eyes were on me. Some had big deer in a headlight eyes while others were cast down or squinty, glaring at me. I sighed. This was going to be a long class, I thought to myself as I took my seat in the back of the room.

The day progressed just as slowly as first period. It was like I was in a zombie movie, and I was the zombie as everything seemed to slow down. Even the constant stares and glares felt like I was being shunned as a pariah. As I ambled down the endless hallway, everyone moved out of my way or flinched when I would pass them. Something was seriously wrong here. I felt like Moses parting the Red Sea, yet it wasn't joyous, it was plain horrible.

Teagan met me at my locker. She had a frown on her face. She must have noticed the change too.

"Aislin, something is wrong. I was sitting in class today and tried to talk to Kona, you know the little pixie with the short black hair and gray eyes, and well she just stared at me and shook her head. Kona loves to chat mostly about the mischief she's gotten into, but today she was as silent as a mouse frozen in fright. That's not like her, Ais, oh and everyone shies away from me like I have the plague."

"I don't know what's going on, Tea, but we will soon find out," I said, as I saw Kaydynce strutting our way.

"What the hell did you do, Aislin?"

Her hands were balled up into fists at her sides. She stared me down like I knew the answer to the problem.

"Um, Kay, I didn't do anything unless you count trying to stop you from killing innocent people." I threw back at her. She shrugged it off like killing someone wasn't a big deal.

"I want to know why everyone is avoiding me. I can't even get a tiny, little taste because everyone flinches away," she fumed.

I would have enjoyed this moment if the same thing weren't happening to Teagan and me. I had no clue how or why this was happening, but I had a hunch of who started it.

"I'd love to stay here and play your little game, Kaydynce, but I have more important things to deal with than you not being able to toy with your food," I said, brushing passed her.

She sniffed, held her head up, shoulders back, and sauntered off with as much dignity as she had left. I took a deep breath and closed my eyes, thinking of where he could be at that moment. My eyes snapped open. *Of course, he's in the library.*

I dashed toward the big double doors. Kaelin may be a jock, but he was one of the smartest guys in our grade so it shouldn't have surprised me to find him chilling in the library with a book in his hands. He had been avoiding me ever since the incident, but that didn't surprise me either. Hell, if I had seen my best friend die, and the person I liked just happened to be there, I'd be asking questions too.

"Hey, Kaelin," I said, as I approached him.

We were the only ones in the library as everyone else had left as soon as they could. He glanced up at me then went back to reading. I slammed my hands down on the table he was sitting at.

"We need to talk."

He laid his book to the side, leaning back in his chair and crossed his arms.

"I'm listening," he said, golden eyes intent.

"I know you're the one behind this," I ground out between clenched teeth.

"Behind what?" he asked coyly.

"You're behind making everyone shun us like we are outcasts or something. No one will talk to Teagan and me, and everyone flinches away if we try talking to them," I accused.

He leaned forward in his chair, resting his elbows on the table, and asked a very simple question, one that I couldn't answer.

"Now why would anyone shun or flinch away from you, Aislin?"

# Chapter 12

I tensed up. Everything inside of me froze. I couldn't answer that question, and it seemed like he knew that already. His golden eyes searched mine. I averted my gaze. I had to answer him, yet I couldn't.

"I-I don't know," I replied, hoping that answer would be good enough.

It wasn't.

"Aislin, please, I've known you almost my entire life. I know when you're lying. You get this pouty look like you're about to cry because you know someone is going to catch your lie. I just want the truth. I've seen a lot of unexplainable things, and I know you know what those things are because it seems like you are always there when it happens."

I gulped. He was right. He was right about everything from my pout to me always being at the scene of the crime. I couldn't fault him for wanting to know the truth, yet I knew he would have a speedier death if he found out the truth about everything.

No one likes a tattletale. Most paranormal beings prided themselves on being undetectable and able to blend into society. Though there were a few whom loved attention and who didn't care if they were found out or not.

"I-I . . . It's complicated," I mumbled.

"It's too complicated to tell your childhood friend? You know, Aislin, I always knew you three were different, yet I could never put a finger on what made you three unlike everyone else. I thought maybe it was your stunning looks, but I now know differently because appearances couldn't kill someone with a kiss." He ran his hand through his hair and shook his head. "She killed him with a single kiss, Aislin. A kiss! I don't know about you, but that doesn't seem normal at all." I opened my mouth, but he cut me off, "You cannot tell me that there isn't something unnatural about her. Or you."

"Kaelin, please, stop searching." Panic constricted my chest. If he kept on like this... "Stop meddling in things you shouldn't or else something bad will happen."

Kaelin pushed himself away from the table and got up, striding over to me.

"What am I meddling in, Aislin?" He towered over me, golden eyes shining. "Hmmm? Can you tell me that?" he asked, raising a brow. I shook my head, throat closing up. He sighed, backing up. "You're included in this, and I will find out what you are hiding."

He turned and stomped off, pushing the double doors with such force that I thought he might actually break it. I groaned and covered my face with my hands. My breath heated my cheeks as I dragged my hands down my face. I already had enough to worry about, but now more things were piling on top of the list. It wasn't enough that I had to deal with a psychotic succubus, but now I had to be even more on my guard as Kaelin snooped around into the supernatural.

I took a deep breath and followed Kaelin out of the library and out into the desolate hallway. All eyes were on me as I shuffled passed all of the students that were still up against their lockers. I hid my face behind my hair as I passed by them. The hair on the back of my neck stood up as everyone stared at me. There was one pair of eyes though that caught my attention. Her wide sapphire ones stared straight into mine as she was towed away by the woman named Celestial and a tall blonde whose hair was bordering on white. Kaydynce struggled in their arms, thrashing her body around like a fish out of water. She glanced all around her like she was hoping someone would save her then her eyes landed back on mine.

I knew immediately that there was no way I could help her even if I wanted to. Both women were extremely muscular despite their lean forms as they lifted Kaydynce off her feet and held her with each one holding an arm. Her eyes pleaded for help as she stared into mine. Her lower lip trembled as her eyes started to well up with tears. She was afraid, and I didn't blame her.

"What's going on?"

I jumped, putting a hand on my chest as I tried to calm my racing heart. I turned toward the source of my scare, Teagan.

"Dang, you scared me, Teagan. I didn't even hear you approach. Anyways to answer your question I have no idea."

She arched an eyebrow and rested her hands on her hips, giving me a look that seemed to say, "are you serious". I shrugged my shoulders glancing back at Kaydynce's retreating form. No one else seemed to notice or even cared that she was being taken away to God knows where. Everyone around us continued on his or her merry way as if nothing had happened.

Maybe nothing had. I would have thought so too if it weren't for the fact that I had seen her carted away. I wasn't the only one. My eyes locked onto his golden ones as his eyelids became slits. Suspicion was written all over his face as he glared from me to the closed door that the three women had left out of.

I sighed. I really didn't want to deal with him at that moment, but it seemed I had no choice as he strode toward me. He grabbed the crook of my elbow and dragged me along with him as he marched away. He didn't stop until we were out of the school and in a secluded area by the picnic tables that were on either side of the school. Many of the students used them as hangouts yet today they were deserted. Everything became deathly silent.

I shivered, rubbing my arms. The air felt chillier like the temperature had dropped a few degrees in a short amount of time. It surprised me that I felt so cold. It was unusual as most banshees could control their internal temperature so the feeling of hot and cold disappeared. I bit my lip. Something wasn't right. I glanced around trying to find the source of the frigidness, yet the only people around were Kaelin and myself.

I glanced back at Kaelin to find him staring at me, his eyebrow arched. Warmth spread up my cheeks at his intense stare. I wanted to look away, but his golden eyes, which reminded me of pools of melted gold, captivated me. Involuntarily I took a step toward him. It was like I was being drawn in, an irresistible attraction. Kaelin must have felt the same, or I had taken more than one step. We were inches apart now, just a hair length away from touching.

"Kaelin, I-I don't want to lose you," I whispered, bowing my head.

I closed my eyes as I felt his hand lightly brush my cheek then lift my chin back up. I opened my eyes slowly as something brush against my eyelashes. I was momentarily caught off guard as I stared into Kaelin's eyes, which were so close that I could see a dark gold ring around his pupil. His eyes lit up at seeing my shock, and I knew he had a grin spreading across his face. I felt the soft touch of his thumb brush against my cheek again. I leaned into it, savoring the feel of his warm, callused palm against my face.

His nose brushed against mine as I inhaled the aroma of autumn and worn leather, his scent. A small smile played across my lips, as I got lost in his eyes. It didn't matter what was going to happen all that mattered was the here and now. I wanted this moment to last forever. I couldn't think of a place I would rather be other than where I was now.

He leaned in even more until our lips met. It was like I was on fire as his sweet kisses became more urgent and needy. His hands moved down to my waist, bringing me closer. I gasped against his lips as all of the air left my lungs.

I was the first to break the kiss, resting my forehead against his, taking in shaky breaths. My heart thrashed against my chest as I tried to gather air into my lungs. Kaelin smiled, staring into my eyes. I smiled back finally feeling happy for a change, but I knew it would never last as the events of the last few days crashed into my thoughts. I knew I shouldn't be doing what I had just done if I was ever going to get over him yet somewhere deep down, I knew there was no getting over him.

I took a couple steps back creating a slight gap between us. Kaelin's brows furrowed, and a frown took the place of his smile as he noticed the gap between us.

"Kaelin, I-I can't do this." Stupid, stupid, stupid...

He took a few steps toward me and lightly put his hands on my forearms, staring down at me with a frown and worry in his eyes.

"Aislin, please, don't push me away. All I want to know is the truth and to understand what the hell is going on. You act like I'm not trustworthy or that I cannot keep a secret since I know you're hiding something, something big." His fingers caressed down my arms as he pleaded his case.

"I know I've been a jerk lately, but we have been friends since we were little kids. I would think that you would trust me by now. After everything we've been through. I would think after all of the secrets that I have kept for you that you would trust me with this one. Please, we can get through whatever it is."

I sighed, bowing my head. He was right like usual. I couldn't deny that we had known each other since we were children or that he had kept every single secret I had ever told him even the one where I admitted that I thought a cartoon character was cute. Best friends didn't keep secrets...even if it's life altering.

"Okay, okay, but promise me that you won't tell a soul what I'm about to tell you because, well, I suppose, because it would put both of us in danger if anyone found out, okay."

# Chapter 13



*Kaydynce*

The world around me was engulfed in darkness. It was like someone had turned off the lights in an unused room. I was a feather in the wind, just drifting, never quite landing. It was unnerving to feel like I was floating in an endless abyss. I knew someone was towing me away somewhere, yet I didn't have an inkling of where I would end up. My body refused to move when I wanted it to as if I was paralyzed.

Could I be dead? I didn't think so. The last thing I remembered was two women hauling me out of the school. I remembered looking for a way out, finding no one I could rely on except the one person I had tried to hurt, Aislin. She did nothing though.

She didn't even try to help me. She just stared at me with her big blue eyes, ugh! My hands clenched into fists as bitterness rose up my throat. She was probably the one who got me hauled away in the first place! I also remembered trying to use my abilities to persuade the women to let me free, but it was like they were immune. Feeling began to come back to my body. Maybe too much as a sharp pain hit my stomach. I ignored it...for now.

Aislin had always been perfect and the most popular despite being younger than Teagan, who used to be the most popular with guys. All I ever heard from classmates and teachers alike was how great Aislin was and how she was the perfect student. It sickened me to the point that I couldn't take it anymore. I was supposed to have all of the attention! I was the prettiest of the three, yet everyone bypassed me and went straight for Aislin. Even her name made me sick. It was like eating a bar of soap because you said a bad word.

My head snapped up at the sound of a creaking door. As the doors were thrown open, I shielded my eyes with my hand as the blinding light shone into the room. I was in either a van or a very dark and damp cell. Neither seemed very likely, but I couldn't be sure. My surroundings were unknown to me except for the brilliant light streaming into my eyes. There was a scuffling then a shadow crossed in front of the light. My eyes adjusted to the sudden change and noticed that the shadow was actually a guy about the same age as me.

He had white hair that fell to his shoulders and eyes so blue that they seemed purple. His clothes were very stylish compared to what I was used to back at school. He had on a dark blue button up shirt and tan dress pants with a white jacket thrown over his shoulder. I smiled sweetly, fluttering my eyelashes. He just stared at me with a blank look on his handsome face. It didn't matter though. He was the first person I had seen since being brought here. It wasn't a bad start to the day.

He held out a pale hand to me, and I took it graciously, smiling up at him as he lifted me off whatever I was standing on. His hand was cold against mine as he led me away. I glanced back and gasped at the sight behind me. Instead of a van or a cell, I had been in some kind of portal, which was actually just an open door with immense darkness inside of it. The door slowly closed then in a blink of an eye it was gone like it had never existed in the first place.

"It's a space in time."

I jumped at the sound of his voice. I hadn't expected him to talk. I glanced up at him to find myself getting lost in his indigo eyes. I tilted my head, studying his features and trying to figure out what he was talking about.

"That doorway you just came out of is a space in time where the accused are held before being taken lawfully to the court," he said, like he was reading my mind.

"What do you mean by accused?" I asked, fearing the answer.

I nibbled on my lower lip as I waited for him to reply.

"I cannot say, only the court can explain the allegations against you," he said, tugging me along.

I wanted to yank my hand away or bring him to a halt so he could explain what the hell was going on. Yet I did none of those things. I just let him lead me to my doom, or at least that was what I presumed by the "accused" part. As we marched, a huge, golden building came into view with tall windows and gargoyles staring down at us. Their red, beady eyes bore into me like they were alive, which it wouldn't surprise me if they were. Beings of that sort did in fact exist despite what some may think.

I took in deep breaths to try and calm my thrashing heart as we hiked up the golden stairs to the archway before the door.

"Ilium Aidan Dreamer and the accused, Kaydynce Ailey Creek," he said, loudly and with authority.

The door slowly creaked open as if it were rarely used or just old and creaky. I studied the boy whom I now knew as Ilium. He had high cheekbones and a pointed chin. It gave him a guise of being malnourished despite looking healthy elsewhere. As if he felt my stare, he turned his head and gave me a curious gaze. It was like he was studying me as much as I was studying him. I was the first to avert my eyes as a slight blush crept up my cheeks.

"Come, we must hurry before the ceremony starts," he said, ushering me inside.

As soon as my feet touched the carpeted floor, the door behind us slammed shut. My head whipped around to stare at it. It was like a gust of wind had blown it closed though I knew that wasn't what had happened. My guess was whoever owned this place had it programmed to close automatically. Ilium hauled me further into the place, down a long hallway, passing door after door. Each door had a different symbol on it and an inscription that I couldn't make out. We strolled down the hallway for a while, never quite stopping until we came upon a magnificent, silver doorway with carvings etched into it.

I reached out a hand and lightly brushed a finger over the etchings.

"This whole place was made by Crain, the greatest wood nymph. She infused the life force of every piece of wood she used to help build this building so that it would continue to stand and live for a lifetime."

I stared in awe at the woodwork and wondered if this place was truly alive and breathing. Suddenly I heard the whisper of music playing just beyond the door. I stared at Ilium. He just nodded and pushed the door open. As soon as I entered, the whole room went wild like a fire was blazing through the chamber. All eyes fell on me, as the crowd grew even crazier. On both sides of the room were rows upon rows of people, and in the middle of the chamber were three seats, which sat two beautiful women and one man. All three of their faces were the same, stiff and harsh.

"Court is now in session." I heard someone say from the far corner of the room.

"Kaydynce Ailey Creek, you are being accused of using your gift on innocent humans without caring about the consequences. You are also accused of killing a boy in front of another human. How do you plea?"

# Chapter 14



"Whoa, hold on, are you saying that all of the legends and myths I've read about are real?" I asked, excited.

Aislin stared at me like I was crazy. Her crystal blue eyes were wide, her lips were in the shape of an O, and her hands were raised like she was about to say something.

"Kaelin, I just told you that I saw your death! Yet you don't even seem concerned? All you can ask is if the supernatural are truly real?"

I laughed. She was cute when she rebuked me for not worrying about my own safety.

"This is serious, Kaelin," she scowled, putting her hands on her hips.

I took a step closer and reached for her hands, holding them in mine. I stared deeply into her eyes, smiling slightly at her scowl. Even when she was mad or irritated, she was still beautiful.

"I know, but that doesn't matter to me right now. All I care about is you in this moment and time. Sure, I might die, someday, but so will everyone else. I just want to live in this moment with you, right now," I said, as my thumbs caressed her hands.

Her blue eyes widened even more as my words sunk in. It was like she was surprised that I wanted to be with her, which was silly after everything we had been through. We had been through thick and thin, always pushing through the good and bad. Suddenly her brows furrowed, her lips crinkled, and her nostrils flared. She crossed her arms over her chest and glared at me.

"Sure, everyone dies, eventually, but you are going to die soon. I have seen your death three times, Kaelin, three times!"

I held her arms down because I knew she would try to emphasize her point with her hands. She was one of those people who talked with their hands.

"Linny, calm down," I said, using the old nickname I had given her when we were little.

Her body tensed. It had been forever since I used that name. When we first met, I had thought her name was weird. It wasn't really a common name. That was also the time when I used my middle name, Quinn, instead of Kaelin.

*"Kaelin O'Neil?" Mrs. Hanes called.*

*"Here, and I go by Quinn," I called back, looking around at my classmates.*

*It was my first day of second grade, and surprisingly I wasn't nervous instead I was excited. It was a new beginning for me, a new start with my dad. It was a chance to finally get to know my dad since I had only been five when he left though later, I found out that my parents had gotten a divorce. The room was filled with scared second graders. Some were shaking like leaves while others fidgeted or tapped their feet. There was one girl though that had caught my attention.*

*She was in the back of the classroom with her head down like she was taking a nap.*

*"Aislin Gray?" Her head snapped up, her chocolate brown hair fanning out around her.*

*"Here."*

*Her voice was like tinkling bells; it was so soft and soothing. All eyes turned to gawk at the brown haired, blue-eyed girl in the back of the room. She shrank down in her seat, hunched her shoulders, and hid her face behind her hair. I smiled to myself. She was kind of cute. Her shyness drew me in. It wasn't until after class that I decided to approach her.*

*Aislin was sitting on one of the benches outside by the playground. It was recess, and I approached her cautiously. She was reading with her legs crossed at the ankles, swinging them back and forth. She was wearing a pale blue T-shirt and jeans that covered her black flip-flops. She seemed oblivious, too absorbed in her book to notice my shadow stealing all her light.*

*"Hi," I said, awkwardly shuffling my feet.*

*She studied me for a second then smiled. Her smile lit up her face. It was like watching the sun rise and warm the earth. Her eyes sparkled like a thousand stars. I was momentarily stunned then she spoke.*

*"Hi, you're Kaelin, right?" she said, her voice like trickling water.*

*I just nodded my head not even thinking that she used my first name or that she even remembered it.*

*"You're Alin, right?" I hoped I was pronouncing her name right.*

*She giggled and shook her head, her long hair moving with her, lightly brushing my hand.*

*"No, it's Aislin, silly."*

*"Aisin?"*

*She laughed again, shaking her head once more.*

*"You know what. I'm going to call you Linny. At least I can pronounce that."*

*She smiled and rolled her eyes. The rest of the day she taught me how to pronounce her name, yet I would always resort back to Linny just to tease her. After that moment we became best friends, inseparable. We were two peas in a pod. We did everything together up until high school.*

"Kaelin, I'm still talking to you, don't ignore me."

I shook out of my thoughts and came face to face with a glaring Aislin. She had her hands on her hips and was leaning in toward me. She still had a scowled on her face.

"Sorry, I got lost in your eyes," I said coyly, grinning.

She rolled her eyes at me, shaking her head, but a smile did grace her lips.

"You're always joking around," she said, laughing.

"It's not a joke though, Aislin," I said, acquiring a serious guise.

She looked at me like a deer caught in headlights. When would she learn that I wanted to be with her? Without missing a beat, I grinned and grabbed her around the waist yanking her in close. She still had a stunned expression on her face, and I took the opportunity to lean in and capture that moment with my lips. At first there wasn't a reaction then like a rocket she was pressed against me, her hands in my hair, and her lips parted. I smiled against her lips, savoring the feel of her soft skin against mine.

I slowly moved my hands from her hips to the inside of her shirt, running my palms against her bare skin. She shivered against me, pressing even closer. I ran my hands up her rib cage, loving how goose bumps rose where my fingers touched then suddenly there was a searing pain in my head. I pushed her away, pressing my hands to my head, and hunched over.

"Kaelin, what's wrong?" Her voice rose in her panic.

I clenched my jaw to hold in the scream that I wanted to let loose. I couldn't let Aislin see how much pain I was in. She would worry too much. Yet something felt different with this pain. It was like someone was calling out to me, but I couldn't receive it from all the pain.

I pushed it down and tried to concentrate on the message. It was one of the hardest things to do, but by the end I was panting for breath. I had finally conquered the pain and with that achievement I heard it. It was a weak voice in the back of my thoughts, yet I heard it all the same. I stared up into Aislin's worried eyes, panting, and told her my findings though it wasn't the news many people would like to find out.

"Kaydynce . . . is in . . . trouble," I breathed, then collapsed letting the darkness engulf me.

# Chapter 15



*Aislin*

He pitched forward. I barely caught him before he hit the ground. He was like a boulder, liable to crush me with all his weight. I lifted him up as much as my small frame could. It was times like these that I wished I had super strength. His body bore down on me, and it was getting harder to hold him up.

"Kaelin, what do you mean Kaydynce is in trouble?" I asked, trying to shake him awake, but he was out cold.

I growled in frustration. This was not how I wanted to end the day. I sighed, my shoulders sagging. I did the only thing I could think of, call for backup. I reached into my pants pocket and withdrew my phone. I dialed the only reliable friend I had left.

"Hey, Teagan, I have a slight problem and need your help. I'm by the entrance to the school next to the picnic tables," I said, then hung up.

She showed up in less than a minute and shook her head at the scene before her. Her eyes were lit up with amusement, something I hadn't seen since Aaron's death.

"How did you manage this, Aislin?" she asked, with one of her eyebrows raised.

"This is not my doing. He just collapsed."

She laughed. "Aislin, people don't just collapse. There is always a reason."

I sighed. "Well, we were . . . talking, and then all a sudden he was hunched over holding his head like it was going to explode. He said 'Kaydynce is in trouble' then collapsed." Teagan shook her head again. Her black curls cascading around her.

"Well, what do you propose we do with him?" she asked, studying me with a small smile on her face.

Heat crept into my cheeks at hearing the suggestion in her words. I shook my head. I couldn't be thinking things like that, not now at least.

"I was thinking of taking him back to my place," I said, then blushed even more.

Teagan's smile grew wider. She was enjoying this.

"I-I didn't mean it like that. I meant we could let him rest at my house while I ask my mom about all of this."

"Mm-hmm, sure. Is that really what you meant, Aislin?" she teased, wagging her brows.

I rolled my eyes. "Can you just help me lift him up, please?"

She nodded, and we both grabbed one of his arms and lifted him so that his arms rested on our shoulders.

"Okay. Now we just have to take him to my car, which is all the way over there," I said, pointing down the long rows of cars to mine.

She looked from my face to where I was pointing. Her eyebrows rose. Her expression was priceless.

"It's not . . . that far," I concluded, shrugging my shoulders, but I also had my doubts.

We started our long trudge with an unconscious Kaelin in tow. Surprisingly after only a few, long minutes we made it to my car without collapsing.

"Well, that wasn't too bad," I said, leaning against my car.
"Yeah, maybe for you since I had most of his weight."
"Well, you're a lot stronger than me."

"Oh, whatever, Aislin, you're just as strong as me," she said, rolling her eyes.

I ignored her, though she was right of course. She was always right. Teagan opened the door to my burgundy Ford, and we both lifted or rather pushed Kaelin's unconscious body into my backseat. He seemed so peaceful, just lying in my backseat though he was knocked out. I shook my head and got down to business. I marched to the driver's side of my car, threw open the door, and got in. I glanced over at the passenger's seat to see that Teagan had already gotten in.

"Okay, buckle up, and let's get this show on the road," I said, backing out of my parking spot.

"Um, Aislin, what show are you talking about?" Teagan asked, raising a brow.

"Oh, you know the one in my head where all the fuzzy bunnies come out to play. What show do you think I am talking about? It's an expression. I just meant let us get this over with."

"Oh, well, why didn't you say that in the first place," Teagan said, shaking her head.

I squinted my eyes, studying her. Something wasn't right, but I couldn't put my finger on it. She seemed too happy. Maybe I was just reading into it. There was nothing wrong with being happy so why was I feeling like something bad was going to happen? I brushed it off and concentrated on the task at hand. I now had to think of a way to explain to my mother why I had an unconscious boy in my back seat, and why I would be bringing him into our house.

We drove in silence the rest of the way, me in deep thought and Teagan, God knows where. It was like she was in a sudden trance. Her curls blew behind her and her green eyes turned glassy. I didn't have time to wonder what the hell was going on with her. I had more pressing issues to deal with. I pulled into my driveway and immediately jumped out, yanking the back door open. I paused for a moment and just stared at his perfection. His red-brown hair was disheveled, yet it was a controlled mess, and it glistened when the sun's rays caught the red tint in its strands.

"Aislin, can I get a little help over here?"

I blinked a few times, coming out of my trance, and looked in my car to the side where Teagan's head was sticking out, glaring at me. I nodded, going around to the other side so that we could both pick him up. With some effort, we managed to haul him maybe a few feet before I heard the door slam. I glanced up to find my mother walking toward us with an expression of disapproval. She just shook her head with a frown on her face.

"I-I can explain," I stuttered.

"No need, I think I know what's going on," she said, as she helped us tow Kaelin inside.

"You do? Well then, please explain it to me because I sure as hell don't understand," I said, plopping down in a chair while my mom and Teagan set Kaelin down on the couch.

"From what I can tell, Kaelin passed out, and I'm guessing it was because of some kind of pain?"

I blinked a few times, lips pursing. "Yeah, he was holding his head, and he was hunched over. He became very breathless then he just collapsed," I replied.

"Did he say anything before he passed out?" she asked, scrutinizing me.

I thought about it for a minute. "Oh yeah, he said Kaydynce was in trouble, but how would he know that?"

Teagan and I both waited for the answer because I knew my mother had the answer. She had that look in her eye like she was hiding something. She took a deep breath then stared directly at me. Her dark blue eyes stared straight into my soul.

"Kaelin was . . . imprinted on in a way," she finally said after a couple minutes.

"What do you mean by imprinted?" Teagan asked, taking a seat in one of the other chairs and scooted it closer.

"Kaydynce left a mark on him. A mark that would allow her to control him, I guess you could say. Yet if what you're saying is true then the mark is faded or wasn't very deep because he fought it, causing his unconsciousness."

"So, what you're telling me is that Kaydynce can use him?" I fumed, balling up my hands into fists.

This was just like her; always doing something stupid that would get her in trouble or wind up dead. I was furious. I took a few deep breaths to try and calm my raging mind. I couldn't believe she would do something like this, well, actually I could. She had been going down this path for a while now. Why did it take me so long to realize? Was I the stupid one? Ugh!

"Aislin, calm down, there are more important matters to discuss," my mother said.

She wrapped a calming arm around my shoulders and gave me a light squeeze. I looked up into her blue eyes and found a hollowness had seen before. Chills ran up and down my spine as an ominous feeling settled in. Her lips quirked up for a split second then thinned out again.

"Kaydynce isn't the only one in trouble, both of you are," she said, her eyes shifting from me to Kaelin, "They know what you have done."

"Wait, what? I don't understand, who knows and about what?"

She looked at me sternly with her jaw set and eyes squinting.

"The court knows of your transgressions and is putting you and Kaelin on trial, though Kaelin will likely be sentenced to death for what he knows."

I stood up, brushing off her arm, and backed away. The room felt smaller as if the walls were caving in on me.

"Wh-Who is the court?" I managed to spit out.

"They are the lawmakers of the supernatural world. Three judges for the three clans, Esor Animi—or soul eater, Nocturna suppression—or nightmare, and then there is Lux Lucis—or light. Each clan has many different supernatural beings included in it like for instance Kaydynce and us would be under Esor Animi, though banshees don't truly eat the soul," Teagan said.

"Hold on, how do you know all of this, Teagan?" I asked, turning toward her and studying her face.

"Well, if you did your history or at least did some research you might have known all of this," she shot back, crossing her arms over her chest.

I winced.

"Teagan is right. There are three clans, and they are

the judges. But what she forgot to mention were the juries who decide if the accused is guilty or not. Most times the ruling will end with the accused being either executed or imprisoned in endless time."

I gulped. Neither of those sounded appealing to me in the least bit.

"So, what does this all have to do with Kaydynce, and also, how the hell did they find out?" I asked, pacing the room.

"Kaydynce was taken today, right?" Teagan said, turning to me.

I nodded. "Yeah, she got hauled away by a woman named Celestial Brook and some other lady."

"She has been taken to the court for judging, and it would not surprise me if they have already come to a verdict. But this is not the time to be worrying about her because they are coming for you, Aislin."

I shivered at the ominous tone of her voice.

"What do I do?" I asked, biting my bottom lip.

"They're here." I heard my grandmother say from the kitchen just as a cold breeze blew the door open.

Three pairs of eyes stared at me then at Kaelin's unconscious body. I ran over to his side, blocking their view. I felt a sense of protectiveness as I stared down three willowy women. Each one had indigo eyes and snow white hair that cascaded down their backs. This was it...

"Aislin Briella Gray and Kaelin Quinn O'Neal come with us for your trial awaits," the three women said in unison.

My heart hammered against my chest as I looked from Teagan's face to my mother's. There wasn't anything either one could do to help me. I glanced down at Kaelin's peaceful face and watched as it contorted into a face of pain. He thrashed around on the couch then sat up, gasping for air. I went straight to his side. I put my hand on his chest, feeling his heartbeat against my palm.

"Kaelin, I'm so sorry," I whispered, before darkness engulfed us both.

# Chapter 16

*Kaelin*

*Save me,* the voice whispered. It was a tickle in the back of my mind, wanting attention. As I focused on the voice, the world came crashing down. There was a sudden flash of light, and a cacophony of noise. I blinked a few times trying to get my bearings as the light intensified. It was like watching one of those movies, where one of the characters would see a light in Heaven, except I wasn't watching it. I was living it instead. The only difference though was I didn't think I was going to Heaven, probably far from it.

*Save me, Dammit!* The voice screamed, its voice reverberating through my head. I put my hands over my ears, pushing away the voice.

*Leave me alone!* I yelled back.

The voice quieted like someone had zipped up its lips. I sighed. Finally. My head still pounded like someone was hitting me with a hammer. The blinding light didn't help either as it burned into my retinas. I held my hands out in front of me and shuffled forward cautiously. My foot lightly tapped something.

I glanced down and could see an outline of a body on the floor. I shielded my eyes and studied the form on the ground. As my eyes adjusted more to the searing light, I saw long brown hair splayed out around a porcelain face, Aislin. My heart stopped. Her pale skin was even paler in the intense light. She looked like a ghost, and she wasn't breathing or at least it didn't seem like it. I bent down on one knee and lightly laid two fingers on her fragile neck, checking her pulse. I let out a deep sigh.

I lightly caressed her soft cheek. She was so beautiful. I smiled to myself then gently nudged her shoulder. Her eyelids fluttered open revealing blue eyes the color of the Caribbean Sea. She blinked a few times then met my gaze. Aislin's eyes widened as she sat up quickly. I put my hands on her shoulders.

"Hey, it's okay. You're fine," I reassured her.

"How long have I been out?" She glanced around the space. Her eyes taking in everything.

"I have no idea," I admitted. "To be honest I just woke up myself."

She nodded and studied my face. "How are you feeling?"

"I'm fine. I'm more worried about you though."

Her brows furrowed as she tilted her head to the side. Her chocolate brown hair fell over her right shoulder. I fought the urge to tuck it behind her ear.

"I-It didn't look like you were breathing and—" I fidgeted under her gaze. "—your skin was paler than usual and... I don't know, it scared me." Fuck...did I just admit that?

"Oh," was all she said as she flipped her hair behind her ear. Damn it, I should have done that.

She nibbled on her bottom lip then cast her eyes toward the light. I could barely see anything through it. It was a major contrast from the darkness that surrounded us.

"What's out there?" I whispered, memorizing her silky skin.

"Judgment."

Goosebumps rose on my arms at that word. I scrunched up my brows, squinting my eyes.

"What kind of judgment?" I asked, searching her face for something.

She wouldn't catch my eye. Instead, she bit her lower lip and messed with her nails.

"Aislin," I said and with feather light fingers lifted her chin. She still averted her gaze. "Please, answer me."

She sighed and met my eyes, tears lining the corners.

"I'm sorry," she whispered. "This is all my fault." Her lips trembled as she continued, "We are being trialed for the secrets I have told you, though I still don't know how they found out." She bowed her head. Strands of hair fell across her face.

"It will be all right," I said, running my thumb over her cheek. Our stance didn't appear so good, though.

"No, it won't. They are going to execute you, Kaelin. A-And I don't know how to save you, not this time."

"Aislin," I said, cupping her cheek, "it's going to be okay. No matter what happens, I will always be with you."

I watched as tears slowly rolled down her cheeks. A tear trickled through my cupped hand. It was like a raindrop falling through my fingers.

"I-I don't want to lose you, Kaelin," she whispered, bringing up her hand to cup one of my cheeks.

"You won't, no matter what," I reassured her, "because I love you, Aislin."

I felt her pulse quicken against my fingertips as she stared into my eyes. I smiled, seeing the surprised expression on her face.

"I-I love you too, Kaelin," she whispered, cupping both of my cheeks and pressed her lips against mine.

I lured her closer, moving my hands down to her waist. She was the first to break the kiss, pressing her forehead against mine.

"I wish we had more time," she sighed as she glanced at the ominous light.

I was about to reply when a hand reached up out of the light and grabbed Aislin's arm, wrenching her away from me. She yelped, her eyes wide and frantic. I scrabbled up, trying to catch her other arm, but I wasn't fast enough. She was ripped away from me.

I jumped through the light, reaching out for her. I was blinded for a second. The first thing I saw was a huge building in the background and someone towing Aislin toward it. I raced after them. My heart pounded through my chest as I ran.

She peered back at me, her hair flying all over the place, with fear in her blue eyes. I pushed myself harder, hoping to catch up with the muscular blond who had Aislin by the arm. I had tried to reassure her, but even I had a fear of losing her. It was a fear that I wished I could just wish away. The man jerked Aislin through the wooden door, and I just barely made it through with my skin still attached.

I followed them through different corridors until we came to a grand door with etchings all through the wood. The guy didn't even look at me as he pushed Aislin through the door and left. She stumbled, almost falling if I hadn't caught her in time. She smiled up at me, but it was a smile that conveyed all the sadness in the world. We strode down the long aisle, feeling the stares of everyone in the room. The walls were lined with chairs full of different beings, all staring at us. It was a little unnerving

We stopped in front of three people. Each were seated in a throne-like chair of the same height. There were two women and a man. Neither of them appeared alike. The woman on the far right had long, raven black hair and pale skin with even paler eyes. The other woman on the other hand had red hair pinned up in a bun and emerald green eyes. The man stood out the most with his ebony skin and lilac eyes. Each one wore an outfit that just said royalty with jewelry on each wrist and hand.

Aislin shook beside me as we waited for one of them to speak. The ebony man's lilac eyes bore into me as he spoke. His voice made the room quake with the power it held.

"Kaelin Quinn O'Neil, you will be trialed on a later date. Today will be the trial of Aislin Briella Gray, and the verdict of Kaydynce Ailey Creek."

I swallowed. This wasn't good. I looked down at Aislin to see flat out panic on her beautiful face. She was petrified as she clung to my arm, her nails digging in.

"It will be okay," I whispered.

Without warning, an arm grabbed ahold of me. I whipped my head around to find the blond, muscular guy. He had a straight face, not a single laugh line could be seen. He tugged me forward, but Aislin wasn't letting go of my arm.

"No, please," she whispered, over and over, eyes shifting around frantically.

Her scream echoed through the room as she was ripped away from me yet again. She screamed in panic and frustration as she struggled against the two men who had grabbed her. I bowed my head in defeat and let him take me away. A door opened in the middle of the room, and I was pushed inside.

"Kaelin!" she screamed again. It was the last thing I heard before the darkness encircled me again.

# Chapter 17



*Teagan*

I strolled through the silent woods feeling lost and alone. Leaves fell softly on the forest floor as I passed. Everything was still as if they were waiting for something to happen. I moved swiftly through the trees, trying to find the perfect spot. My heart hammered against my chest as I thought about what I was going to do. It had to happen, and I wasn't afraid.

The trees were painted an off white as the full moon shone through the barren branches. Each step took me closer to the end, but hopefully to a new beginning. The silence enticed me as if to say, "You can do it". It felt like a shroud was being thrown on top of me, yet it didn't have that suffocating feel. I embraced it. I stretched out my fingers and brushed them along passing trees, feeling the roughness of each trunk.

As I ambled on, I thought back on my life and how I had gotten to this point. I sighed, closing my eyes and lifting my chin to bask in the moon's light. A light breeze tickled my hair, coaxing it to lift in the wind. Strands of my hair reflected off the moon's rays, casting their own shadow. My life had been perfect, for a while at least. Then it all came crashing down on my eighteenth birthday. Ironic how I had finally become an adult then my world caves in like it was just waiting for that moment.

I felt betrayed by the world and my being. Nothing made sense except that I had known it would happen since my birth. Life is a bitch. I hated myself, and the world for the pain I had to go through, yet I had my friends by my side. Despite falling into the depths of despair, I had come out alive. I had let go of my grief and tried to live as best as I could, but of course God or whatever, throws me a curve ball. I found love again after thinking it was lost to me, though in all actualities, it truly was. I could never truly love again for my love has a death sentence.

Aaron's death was the breaking point for me. I had lost everything except the ones who had been there for me through thick and thin. I couldn't fall back into the depths for I would be lost completely. If I fell, then what I was about to do would be for nothing. I couldn't do that to them. They needed me, and I would be damned if I didn't come through.

I pushed those thoughts away, focusing on the here and now. I stopped, taking in my surroundings, and sat down on a clear spot in the middle of the woods. The clearing was an open space with trees surrounding it like a circle. Not a single leaf touched the inner circle. That is when I knew I had found the spot. I lay back, stretching out my whole body, and looked up at the night sky. It was beautiful. The darkness shone with a billion stars that seemed to light up the world if only for a moment.

I took two deep breaths, centering myself, and then withdrew the blade. It was a switchblade of multiple colors. It changed from blue to green then to pink and purple. Cole had given it to me on my eighteenth birthday. That was also when I had my first Death Call. He had even had it inscribed. *To my little teapot.*

*"Hey, teapot, I got you something."*

*His voice whispered against my skin. I lifted my eyes to stare into his chocolate brown ones. His lips sprung into a grin as he held out a box.*

*"You didn't have to get me anything."*

*"I know, but it's your birthday. I wouldn't be a good boyfriend if I didn't get you something."*

*I laughed and took it from his hands. The box was silver with a green bow on top. I lifted the lid and peeked inside. I smirked seeing a switchblade.*

*"I thought you might need it to keep away the other boys and girls."*

*I rolled my eyes and reached for the knife. As soon as my fingers brushed against it, I screamed. My first Death Call was of him ripped to shreds, screaming as the wolf tore him apart.*

I squeezed my eyes shut as the first teardrop slide down my cheek. I swallowed a couple of times, trying to calm myself. The moon bore down on me from above, and I knew it was time.

I did it as quickly as I could. I winced as the cold metal sliced through my skin like butter. I watched as blood trickled down my arms to pool beneath me. I stared at the ruby red liquid, watching it turn into two mini ponds. I felt lighter like I was a feather being lifted by the wind. I wondered if this was what it felt like to be free, unbounded. As my life force slowly waned, I thought about why I was doing this and the warning I had received.

*"Teagan, there is something you must do, and only you can do it," Mrs. Gray whispered, once we were alone.*

"What must I do?" I asked, feeling a sense of foreboding. She whispered it into my ear. I gasped, backing away from her.

"I-I cannot." I blinked then hung my head. "I mean it's crossed my mind, but I would never do that."

"You would still say no if it meant losing your friends?" she asked, raising a brow. I stared at her, unsure of how to answer. "You are the only one who can save them, Teagan. It must be you for you have the most sorrow in your heart and soul."

"I-I don't understand what that would achieve," I whined. Suicide? That had to be another way...

"Your true form, Teagan. Our kind was never truly meant to live among the living. We are the omens, foretellers of death. Very few know of this, but a banshee has two forms: a human and spectral. There is only one way to reach our true form, but there are cautions you must take. Our spectral form has some advantages, but there are also downfalls.

"In spectral form you can appear and disappear at your will, allowing you to go places others cannot. However, there are forces that would love to control that power. I believe you have met one of them, the wraith. He is a very powerful being who feeds off the sorrows of others." Her dark eyes bore into mine.

"Wait, so you are saying if I become my true form then I can go anywhere I please?" I asked, making sure I had heard her right.

She sighed. "Yes, but there is a certain way you must do it. There is a full moon tonight, which is what you will need, and you will need to be strong. There was only one other banshee who reached her true form though it was on accident. She fell into the hands of the wraith and became what many think of when we hear the term banshee. She was so wrecked by her grief that she left herself open to darkness.

*"You must focus and not be distracted by your grief. Use your sorrow to become your true self." She spread her arms out wide. "Metamorphosize!"*

I nodded my head, settling my despair into a target. I concentrated on my task at hand, using my grief as a motivator. The light consumed me as the short life I had lived finally ended.

# Chapter 18

*Aislin*

"Kaelin!" I screamed, thrashing against the guards that held me at bay, "This isn't how it's supposed to happen."

My body went limp as Kaelin blinked out of sight. He was gone, probably for good. The guards around me disappeared like I had imagined them. My eyes blurred as tears clouded my vision. I blinked them away. I refused to let the court see me cry.

I pushed back all my feelings and glared at the three in front of me. The redhead smiled, her fangs glistening in the pale light. I shuddered as the room temperature dropped a couple of degrees. I was momentarily stunned as the cold played across my skin. My fingers went numb at the tips. It surprised me, as banshees were able to control their body temperature.

This wasn't a natural cold. It was the same feeling I had back at the school and then again at my house. The court had been there all along, waiting and watching my every move. My blood boiled at the thought. Was there no such thing as privacy?

"Bring in the first accused!" the ebony man boomed.

The room temperature dropped even more as ice started to form on the railings, forming long and pointed icicles. The side doors flew open with a bang, revealing Celestial Brook along with her partner, the blonde, and then Kaydynce. All eyes fell on the one in the middle, Kaydynce. She looked like crap. Her short blond hair stuck out everywhere, and her skin seemed even paler. She wore the same thing she had at school: denim mini skirt and a bright pink, low cut shirt. She may have been wearing the same clothes, but they were torn and tattered.

Her usually lively eyes were dull and forlorn. Her pink lips had turned a sickly blue as the temperature continued to drop. I shivered even more, my teeth chattering. The temperature had dropped so much that I could see my breath. It was like a heavy fog hung there.

"Can someone please turn up the heat in here?" I asked, motioning at the icicles forming on the railings to get my point across.

"You may speak only when spoken to, Ms. Gray," the black haired woman said, her pale eyes glowing.

Her eyes bore into me like she was seeing right down to my soul. I had the irrational thought to cower in fear, but I knew better. Showing fear was one of the worst things to do around a predator. I lifted my chin and stared directly into her eyes. I wouldn't show any fear no matter what. She could go screw herself.

"Court is now in session!" the ebony man boomed.

The room quieted as everyone settled down and waited for the judgment to be made.

"It is time to hear from the accused," the red-haired woman said.

She stood up and motioned to Kaydynce first.

"How do you plea, Ms. Creek?" she asked, with a glint in her green eyes.

"Not guilty, of course!" Kaydynce cried, struggling against her captives.

"So, you deny draining an innocent human in front of another human?" the woman on the right asked. Her long, black hair swaying as she shifted.

"Well, I-I . . . It wasn't like that," she stuttered.

"We have heard enough," the man boomed. "It is now time to hear what the jury thinks."

"Wait! she didn't even get to defend herself! How is that even fair?" I cried out, gulping as all eyes fell on me.

"Ms. Gray, I will not tell you again, you may only speak when spoken to," the black haired woman warned.

I brushed off her warning. This was not fair. She didn't even have time to defend herself before being judged.

"I will not back down." I turned toward the crowd, "I don't believe she can be judged on just one crime. Everyone makes mistakes or bad decisions. Is it fair to judge someone from that one instant? I know Kaydynce has done wrong, but she has also done good in her life. She has been my friend since we were little. I could always trust her no matter what. I mean sure she got on my nerves occasionally, but that doesn't mean she should be judged unfairly."

The black haired woman stood up and motioned to someone in the back. I was quickly restrained again. I didn't fight. What would be the point? I probably screwed both of our chances of getting out alive, yet I had to voice my opinion. I just hoped we could make it through.

"I have heard enough of this," she said, "Jury, your verdict?"

A short, blond boy stood up from the crowd. He had milky eyes and wore a plaid jacket that seemed to engulf his whole body.

"We find the accused guilty of all charges," he said, his voice wispy like the wind.

The redhead woman smiled. Her fangs gleamed along with her emerald green eyes. Something was about to happen.

"Take the accused to the abyss," the ebony man rumbled.

My heart sped up as my breath quickened. I looked over at Kaydynce to see the same expression of fear in her eyes. I had to do something, anything to save her even though she did try to kill Kaelin. I thrashed against my restraints, kicking one of them in the privates. I was released momentarily, and I took that opportunity to run toward Kaydynce. I had to think fast because quite frankly I had no clue what I was doing.

"Ilium, open the abyss," the black haired woman ordered.

I had barely made it to her before the floor opened under us. It was like jumping off a bridge without a safety line. Our screams echoed through the courtroom then there was nothing.

We floated in the darkness like leaves falling gently. Everything around me was completely black. I could barely see Kaydynce. It was like someone had put a blindfold over my eyes in which you could see outlines but nothing else.

I fanned my arms out in front of me trying, relentlessly, to reach Kaydynce. It was like there was a barrier between us.

"Kaydynce, are you there?" I called out.

"Aislin, I'm scared," she cried.

"It's going to be okay, Kay, we will get out of this," I reassured her, though I was skeptical.

I didn't know how the hell we were getting out of this, but that wasn't the only problem. As I floated through the darkness, I heard the moans and cries of others that had been sent here as well. We weren't the only ones hoping to get out.

# Chapter 19

*Kaydynce*

The air around me hummed with excitement yet I couldn't fathom why. We were trapped, every single one of us. I was surrounded by supernatural beings, but I couldn't see any of them, just feel their presence. I didn't know how long I had been stuck in this darkness, and I had no clue if I would ever get out. I wanted to blame someone, anyone, for being in this mess yet I knew it wasn't anyone else's fault but mine.

Voices reverberated through the abyss, echoing continuously. I covered my ears trying to block out the noise, yet it was futile. Sound kept on filtering no matter what I did. Suddenly, pain stabbed through my stomach though at this point I wasn't even sure if I had a stomach much less an actual body. My stomach burned, as if I was being seared from the inside. I needed to feed, badly. The only way I could get what I needed was to find a way out of this hellhole.

My head snapped up as I felt the presence of someone new. I wasn't the only one who noticed. Fidgeting and the rustle of clothing could be heard as everyone in the abyss shifted, hoping to catch a glimpse of the newcomer. The voices around me rose in excitement. I covered my ears with my hands, trying to block out the noise. I growled, balling them up into fists.

"Shut up. Shut up. SHUT UP!" I screamed, hunching over.

I rocked on my heels, wishing everything would disappear. Though in all actuality I was completely alone except for the continuous complaining of the others locked in the utter darkness with me. This place was messing with my head. For a moment I thought I heard the voice of Teagan, but that was impossible, as she wasn't stuck in this place. I shook my head, thinking I had just imagined it. My head snapped back up as I heard my name. I followed the voices, hearing my name being repeated. I focused onto the conversation at hand.

"We can't just leave her." I heard Aislin say.

"She tried to kill Kaelin and me! How can you forget that?"

"I'm not denying that she did those things, but that doesn't mean we should leave her here."

"Why not? if she could leave us here, she would, without a second thought—and you know it just as much as I do."

Even though I couldn't see either one of them, I knew Teagan had her arms crossed over her chest and giving Aislin a stern look.

"Despite what she has done, she is still our friend," Aislin said. *Oh simple, Aislin...*

"Fine, but if she tries anything I swear I'll haunt you both."

The voices of both Aislin and Teagan just suddenly stopped. Had I imagined it? I shook off the thought. Maybe I was just having a nightmare, and all I needed to do was wake up. I pinched my arm, hoping beyond hope that I would wake, but nothing happened. I was still stuck in this dark abyss, forever surrounded yet utterly alone.

I pondered on the words that may have or may not have been real. Aislin still thought of me as a friend despite everything I had done. I didn't know how I felt about that. I didn't know if I should feel humbled or straight out disgusted. Teagan was right. I had put myself before anyone else, and I was damn proud of that. The only person you could truly trust is yourself.

*Aislin is too weak and trustworthy, which will be her down fall,* I thought to myself, smiling.

Suddenly there was a whooshing sound and a flexing of the darkness around me. Then out of nowhere Teagan appeared. She didn't look right. She was even paler, and she had this soft glow around her. She extended her right hand, which appeared translucent.

"Grab my hand, Kaydynce. I may not want to but I'm saving your sorry ass," she said, waving her hand in front of my face.

I hesitated, putting my hands on my hips and narrowing my eyes. I didn't trust her, but she was the only way out. I took her hand cautiously, and as soon as I did a slow fog crept around us. Then in a blink of an eye, I was back in one of the many corridors. Both Teagan and Aislin were beside me. Teagan had a frown etched into her purplish blue lips while Aislin had a broad smile, lighting up her eyes.

"Okay, we have one more stop to make. We need to save Kaelin before his trial," Aislin said, glancing from me to Teagan.

"Aislin, I can't," Teagan said, with downcast eyes.

"What do you mean you can't?" she asked, her smile fading. "You got us out. It should be a piece of cake getting him out."

"What I mean is I have no clue where he is or where to find him. He is human, Aislin, my powers only work for the supernatural."

Aislin stiffened at those words. Ha.

"Then we have to search for him. We can't just give up." She threw her hands into the air then pointed at Teagan's spectral form. "**I** was the one who got him into all this mess, so I OWE HIM!" she fumed.

I watched as they bickered back and forth. It reminded me of one of those comedy shows with husband and wife where they always fought about meaningless things. I sighed.

"I might know someone who could help," I suggested. I didn't even know why I was helping them. Maybe it was the fact that they had actually saved me, though given a little more time I probably could have escaped by myself.

The minute I spoke, two pairs of eyes stared at me. One pair was wide with hope while the other was narrowed in suspicion. I knew Aislin would win out: even though Teagan was the oldest Aislin had always been the leader of the group.

"We can't trust her," Teagan whispered.

She glared at me. Her eyes narrowed even more. I smiled, fluttering my eyelashes.

"If she knows someone who can save Kaelin then I'm up for it."

Teagan sighed, shaking her head and mumbled, "Of course you are." But didn't argue anymore. Aislin had won like always.

"All right, let me go find him," I said, starting to walk off.

I saw out of the corner of my eye Teagan about to rush forward, but Aislin held her back. It was like Teagan was a dog and Aislin had the leash. I laughed to myself picturing Teagan as some kind of dog. I had to shake the image so I could focus on the task at hand. I had to find Ilium. I skipped down the corridor as if I hadn't been just locked up. I played with my hair as I contemplated how I was going to finish the task I had put forth for myself. I did the only thing I could think of when people search for someone.

"Ilium?" I whispered, not expecting it to actually work.

"You called?" he said, popping out of nowhere.

I turned around quickly finding myself face to face with a tall, white-blond haired boy. He appeared healthier this time.

"Hi," I said, unable to think of what I needed to say or ask.

My mind blanked. It was like the minute I laid eyes on him I lost all thought and reason. I never expected to feel this way. My heart fluttered against my chest as I looked up into his indigo eyes. His lips curled up into a smirk, eyes dancing. I gulped. It felt like I was seeing a whole other person from the one that had taken me to my trial.

"Was there something you needed?" he asked, his eyes glimmering in the pale light.

I felt compelled to take a step toward Ilium like someone was pulling an invisible string, bringing me closer. I was a moth drawn to a flame.

"I-I wanted to ask for a-a favor," I said, hesitantly.

If he was what I thought he was, then that meant I needed to tread lightly.

"Oh, a favor, and what kind of favor were you searching for?" he asked, with one eyebrow raised.

I tucked my hair behind my ear, biting my lip.

"Well, my favor is for you to free a human who was locked up recently. His name is Kaelin O'Neil," I said.

I bit my lip harder in my nervousness, drawing blood. His hand shot out quickly then vanish from my view.

I was momentarily stunned yet mesmerized as I watched Ilium lick a drop of blood off his finger. His indigo eyes lit up, taking on a glassiness. For some reason, heat coursed up my neck and cheeks. I felt flustered, like I was burning up.

Everything on my body felt like it was on fire. I didn't know if it was my hunger kicking in again or something else entirely. My breath came in small gasps as I noticed Ilium's close proximity. We were only inches apart. I could feel his breath on my cheeks, moving my hair softly. His chilled body only made mine warmer.

"I shall do this favor for you, Kaydynce Creek, and in return you must do a favor for me as is customary," he said, with a glint in his eyes.

He reached out a hand and lightly brushed my cheek. I sucked in a breath at his feather light touch. My heartbeat quickened as I stared into Ilium's purple eyes.

"Do you accept?" he asked, running a finger down my cheek.

I closed my eyes just for a second, savoring his touch. His finger left a trail down my cheek to my lips.

"Yes," I whispered against his index finger.

"Then I shall save this human, and in return you shall come back home with me," Ilium said, a smile slowly spreading across his lips.

"Where is that?" I asked, tilting my head to the side.

"The other world is where my home is, where the supernatural can live in peace."

"May I ask what kind of supernatural being you are?"

He smiled and tucked his long hair behind his ear. His ear was pointed at the tip.

"I am an elf," he said, "though you seem to already know that."

"I had my suspicions," I said, smiling mischievously.

He grinned down at me then in an instant his pale lips were meddled against mine. I was shocked for a moment then fell into his arms, which encircled my waist. My hunger resurfaced with a gnawing ache, and I couldn't help myself. I needed to feed. At first it was a slow tug then in an instant it was like a dam opening. His life force flowed into me, and it was delicious. It tasted of strawberries and marshmallows cooked over a campfire. Then just as it came it was gone. Ilium created a gap between us.

I wanted to taste his essence again. It was like nothing I had ever tasted. A whimper escaped my lips.

"You shall have more later, my sweet," he said, pressing a finger against my mouth.

I nodded like a little kid who was told they could have a cookie after dinner. I wanted more, but I knew I had to wait.

"I shall find this human for you and keep him safe until you can protect him yourself," he said.

Then just like that he was gone like he had never been there in the first place.

# Chapter 20

*Aislin*

My heart stopped the minute I saw Kaydynce without Kaelin. I wanted to scream and yank my hair out. Where was he? Were we too late? I couldn't think about that now. I had more pressing issues to deal with. I bit my lower lip as I watched Kaydynce saunter closer.

"I knew we couldn't trust her," Teagan whispered in my ear.

Her green eyes were in slits as she stared at the approaching form. I couldn't blame her. Kaydynce had tried to kill her, that would be cause for mistrust. Maybe I was just too forgiving, but I believed everyone should have a second chance. Despite being hopeful, I still had my doubts about if Kaydynce truly came through for us.

The pale walls seemed to cave in on me as my heart sped up, as Kaydynce got closer and closer. I took two deep breaths to try and calm myself. This wasn't like me. I rarely ever got worked up especially since I had to be somewhat of the leveled one though Teagan usually took over that job.

"Where is he?" I asked, feeling slightly frantic.

I chewed on my lower lip and looked around the hallway hoping he might pop out to try and scare me, but it didn't happen. Instead, I was left staring at Kaydynce and the empty spot beside her.

"He is safe. I have someone keeping a close eye on him, don't worry," she said, flipping her blond hair like it was nothing.

I gnawed on my lip, still worried. If he weren't safe, then it would be my fault. I was the one who had gotten him into this in the first place.

"Come on, Aislin, it's time to go before someone catches us," Teagan said, jerking on my arm.

"I can't," I said.

"What?" Teagan and Kaydynce said in unison.

"What do you mean you can't?" Teagan asked.

"I can't just leave them here."

"The hell you can," Teagan growled, tugging even harder on my arm.

"They are just as trapped as we were, stuck in complete darkness, Teagan. I can't in good conscience leave them," I said, staring at the wall we had come from.

"We need to leave, Aislin, we can't save them," Kaydynce chimed in, reinforcing Teagan.

My heart sank at the realization that maybe I wouldn't be able to save all these supernatural beings. I sighed, and then an idea struck me.

"Wait, Kaydynce, what about your friend or whatever?"

The moment I mentioned her friend, she tensed. Her blue eyes narrowed, and a frown formed on her pink lips.

"No."

"What do you mean no?" I whined.

"You don't know what you are asking, Aislin."

"I cannot leave them here, Kaydynce, just like I couldn't leave you. Please, if your friend can help them then ask him." "Fine, but I warned you," she said, then called out a name.

Her words hung in the air as silence filled the hallway. All was still as we waited for something to happen. Then in a blink of an eye, we weren't alone. A tall, lean, white haired guy stood between Kaydynce and me.

"You called, my lady," he said, bowing toward Kaydynce.

Kaydynce sighed. "My...friend, Aislin, she wants to... ask a favor."

The newcomer turned toward me and smiled, his purple eyes lighting up. I shivered, feeling the hairs on my arm and neck stand up. I brushed off the feeling, thinking maybe I was imagining it.

"What kind of favor are you asking?" he said, staring into my eyes.

"I-I want to free everyone from this place and to not have to worry about being chased down by the court again," I said, biting my lip.

"You know that is two favors, right?" he said, smiling, "Two favors require two returned favors. Do you still wish to continue?"

I gulped. Did I really want to do this? I didn't know what the favors would require; yet I knew I had to do something.

"Yes," I said, letting out a deep breath.

"Very well, I shall free everyone, but know this, not everyone was put in there for mundane things."

There was a whooshing sound then a thousand doors appeared out of nowhere, all of them closed. I was confused for a moment. Were they free? Shouldn't the doors be open? I had many questions.

Then like he was reading my mind, the doors flew open. Every single one, banging against the walls. As soon as the doors opened, every shape, color and size came rushing through, pushing and shoving each other to freedom. Some had horns on their heads while others had them on their arms. Then there were some who had glowing skin and fins all over their bodies.

Some of the beings that scurried out of the doors were like nothing I had ever seen yet there were some, which anyone could recognize. Vampires, pixies, and werewolves came barging pass everyone. The pixie's pale, veiny wings fluttered and twitched causing it to swoop and rise then swoop again. Every single being appeared ragged and weak, even their clothes were tattered.

I second-guessed my decision as I locked eyes with a male vampire who had spiky black hair and silver eyes. He licked his lips, and I saw his incisors lengthen. His eyes turned a blood red as his hunger took over.

He dashed toward me, moving swiftly through the crowd. I barely had time to react before he was upon me.

His pale hands grabbed my shoulders and drew me in close. I could feel his breath on my face as he whispered, "I hope you taste as sweet as you look."

He tilted my head to the side and slowly kissed my neck. I shivered against him. Then just before he would take his first bite, I was slung backwards. When I lifted my eyes, I saw the blond guy in my place except he had the vampire by the throat, lifting him up above the crowd. It was like watching a superhero crush his enemy. He then threw the vampire across the hallway. The vampire hit the wall and crumbled into a broken heap.

"I warned you, young banshee, not everyone is as innocent and trustworthy as you think. I shall keep our bargain as long as you do, and in doing that you must stay alive. If you are dead then how would I get my favor," he said, turning his head and smiling down at me.

"Thank—," I started to say before Kaydynce cut me off. "Come on. Let's go before someone else tries to eat us."

I nodded, about to follow the mob, when I noticed another being cautiously creeping out of one of the doors.

# Chapter 21

*Remy*

Light crashed down on me as I passed through the open door. I shielded my eyes and stared in wonder at my surroundings. Everything was slowly coming into view as my eyes adjusted to the brilliant light. As my eyes adjusted, I noticed four figures just standing there, staring at me. One of them approached me. She had long, dark brown hair, and clear blue eyes that seemed to take in everything. I met her eyes timidly, feeling like I had just interrupted something.

"It's all right, you're free now. You don't have to be afraid," she said, smiling sweetly.

I nodded slowly as I felt my body finally start to feel like itself again. The darkness had stunted my appetite for the time, and now it came crashing back. I crumbled to my knees, holding my stomach. I gasped in pain, feeling my stomach turn inside out. It was like my body was eating itself just to survive. I heard the popping of joints as the girl crouched down in front of me. I felt her stare and looked up into two pools of crystal blue water. I pushed up my glasses, feeling heat rush up my cheeks at her never faltering stare.

"Ma'am," I croaked, then cleared my throat, "do you know what year it is?"

She tilted her head and squinted.
"It's 2014."

My heart sunk. I had been in that claustrophobic darkness far longer than I had thought. It felt strange to ponder on the thought that the world might have changed. I wasn't surprised though. Things never seemed to stay the same. My life had done the same thing, changed in an instant.

"Do you know where you are?" another voice asked.

I turned my head toward the voice and stared into squinted dark green eyes. The eyes were the only striking thing about the spectral form. There were feminine qualities to this ghost, but it was hard to tell as her form flinted in and out of existence. Her once colored hair had turned a misty gray, blending into her body.

"Of course, I am at—," I paused, losing my train of thought. It was like someone had stripped the memory of where I had been held, "actually, I am not sure. I have a gap where I thought the memory was stored."

I watched as a frown formed on both of their lips.

"Your mind has been wiped clean of the memory of the court," a deep voice said.

My head snapped to the other side of the blue-eyed girl. My eyes landed on a long, pointed face with dark purple eyes. He had long, white hair that fell to his waist.

"What do you mean, sir?" I asked, puzzled.

"As a precaution, the court takes away the memory of ever being here," he then looked over at the women, "neither one of you were in the abyss long enough for them to extract anything."

"What's your name?" the blue-eyed one asked.

"It's Remy, Remy Jackson, ma'am."

"Well Remy, I'm Aislin, and this is Teagan," she motioned toward the specter, "and that's Kaydynce," she said, pointing to another woman I hadn't noticed.

She had short, blond hair and eyes that shone like sapphires.

"And I am Ilium," the last of them said.

I nodded, trying to remember each of their names in turn. The twinge of hunger was a constant reminder of how long I had been locked away.

"Can you tell us how you got here?" the woman called Aislin asked.

"Aislin, that is a personal subject. Why would you ask that? He had already been through enough," the ghost scolded. Teagan, Teagan was her name. I had to put faces to the names.

"It's all right, ma'am, I don't mind telling everyone my past, though it's a sad one," I warned.

"It all started in the year of 1863, the year my life changed forever. The Civil War had started by then. I, at the time, was also a slave. I had been one ever since my birth.

What I didn't know at the time was what I was, a wizard."

*"Remy!"*

*I smiled to myself as I heard Nereida's singsong voice calling to me from across the pond. She was on the other bank, sunning herself. Her long, pink hair swayed behind her as she turned to stare at me. Her eyes were the color of rough water during a storm, a dark smoky blue. Her long, iridescent sea green tail flicked and slapped back down, trying to get my attention. Water droplets glistened off her gorgeous body.*

*"Nereida, you know I'm not supposed to be here. I need to get back to work before your father catches me with you." Her lush lips turned down into a pout.*

*"Awe, come on, you can muck out the stalls later," she said, beckoning with her index finger.*

*I sighed, shaking my head as I waded through the pond to the other side. Nereida smiled, her eyes lighting up.*

*"So, what should we do now?" she whispered, turning on her side as I approached.*

*"Well, since you persuaded me over here, I think I will take advantage of that and do this," I said, leaning down and capturing her lips with mine.*

*I felt her body shift underneath me. A gentle breeze passed over us, chilling my wet legs. We were too engrossed in each other to care about the outside world. Her skin heated up under my touch, initiating the change. Her once corral pink hair morphed into a red, the color of leaves in the fall.*

*Nereida's tail shifted into the most beautiful set of legs. I kissed her deeper, feeling her lips part against my tongue. I pressed my body closer to her. Her heartbeat sped up as her cheeks turned the lightest shade of pink.*

*I smiled against her lips as my hands roamed over her figure. Our lips broke apart as I took in a big gulp of air. Unlike Nereida, I needed air to breathe. The moment my lips left hers, they were off to another part of her body. My lips traced a path from her lips to her belly.*

*"You know your transformations are quite convenient," I mused. My eyes admired her nakedness.*

*"I'm so glad my nakedness appeases you," she teased.*

*"It does, very much so," I whispered against her thighs.*

"That was the last treasured moment I had with her. The next day, August 21, I was enlisted to take the place of my master in a raid for the Confederates. I didn't know it at the time, but that would be the last day I ever saw my Nereida."

*"Remy, you cannot do this," Nereida said, breathing heavily.*

*"I must. Your father has made it an order. I cannot say no. I have to do this."*

*"If you do this, then you will be fighting for the continuation of slavery," she huffed, lifting and fooling with her green, puffy dress.*

*"Reida, I cannot disobey your father," I said, cupping her cheek.*

*"Please, Remy, I have a bad feeling about this," she begged, pleading with her eyes.*

*"I won't be gone long. It's only one town over. I will come back to you, I promise," I said, leaning down and capturing her supple lips.*

*"Remy," a deep voice called from outside the house.*

*"I have to go before your father gets out the whip again," I said, taking a step back.*

*I was about to walk away when she brought me in close again.*

*"I love you," she whispered against my ear.*

*"I love you too," I whispered back then kissed her once more.*

*I left her standing there as I went into the unknown. Nereida's father was waiting for me as I stepped outside. Mr. Ross wasn't a big man. In fact, he was one of the shortest I had ever met. He was referred to as a dwarf. He had dark brown eyes, dark brown hair, and a long, pointed beard that was about the same color brown as his eyes. Instead of working in the mines like most dwarves, Mr. Ross made his livelihood growing crops. He didn't use the conventional methods though. He worked underground making sure the crops grew properly.*

*"Go get my horse, Remy, and meet the others by the hickory woods."*

*"Yes, sir," I said, running off to the stables to saddle up Mercy.*

*Mercy was a thoroughbred mare, which could run like the wind if she chose to. I saddled her up. Glad Mr. Ross had given me riding lessons. I met the raiders by the woods, and we set off toward our destination. I had known the raiders for a little over a month now, yet I didn't know a single one of their names. Each was just as rugged as the next. The only differences were the color of their hair and beards.*

*I wasn't the only colored man in the raid, in fact, there were two others. There were over fifty raiders, all on horses. Some rode chestnuts while others had dappled grays and black mares.*

*The horses nickered and whinnied to each other as we rode through the woods to the other side. The leaves on the trees were just barely starting to change their colors as fall approached. The forest floor was alive with the noise of hooves crunching leaves and fallen branches.*

*We jumped over logs, fallen trees, and streams as we made our way to our destination. The leader of the group slowed, holding up a hand to halt us as we approached the edge of the forest. I glanced around, catching the eyes of some of my partners. Worry and fear crossed many of their faces as we looked down at the town below us. There were a few men milling about towing logs, harvesting crops, and chatting with others. There were also a few women. Children ran around, laughing in glee, without a care in the world.*

*At that moment it felt wrong to attack a town so defenseless, unfair. I didn't know if I could through with it. I would have copped out then, but at that moment the leader raised his sword and pointed it forward.*

*"Charge!" he yelled, as he kicked his horse into action.*

*I couldn't back out now, I thought as everyone around me charged on forward. I nudged Mercy into action and followed the crowd. The screams of women, men, and children were the first things I heard then the bang of a gun firing off. After the first shot, I heard more. The smell of gunpowder and the metallic scent of blood mingled together as dust and smoke blew through the air. I watched as bodies fell in slow motion, as blood spewed from their lips and chests.*

*Both Confederate raiders and Union townsmen fell as shots continued to fire from both sides. As I rode through the town, one of the townsmen charged me with a pitchfork. Without thinking, I slammed the butt of my gun into his forehead. He fell backwards, dropping his weapon. I let out a sigh of relief as I felt my heart thrashing against my chest. The fight wasn't over though. The battle was still raging on around me, but I didn't notice as a familiar figure rode toward me. I would have recognized her anywhere despite the men's clothing and the hat that hid her long, red hair.*

*I called out her name, motioning her back the way she came, and that was when it happened. I saw it all happen in slow motion. She was riding toward me, still a few yards away, when one of the townsmen snatched a gun away from a fallen raider and raised it up, cocking it back, and then fired. I kicked Mercy into action, but I wasn't going to make it in time. I watched as the bullet hit Nereida directly in her chest. She fell backwards, her hat falling off. Her body fell gracefully to the ground, her hair splayed out around her.*

*I jumped off Mercy as soon as I got close enough to her body. I ran toward her and got down on my knees, cradling her head in my lap.*

*"Reida, please don't leave. Don't leave me alone," I whimpered, holding her close.*

*"I . . . will always . . . be with . . . you," she rasped out.*

*Her once beautiful voice croaked and cracked as the life slowly drained out of her. Blood bubbled up her throat as she coughed. Blood trickled out of her lush lips. Her pale skin became even paler and cold.*

*"Nereida," I cried.*

*"Good-bye, my love," she whispered as her eyelids fluttered closed.*

*"No. Please, no!" I yelled, shaking her, trying to wake her back up.*

*It was no use. She had already left this world. I felt hot, tears stream down my face and rage boil up inside me. White, hot, lightning sparked through my body, and all I saw was red. The* burning started in my chest then traveled all over my body until it hit my hands. The heat coursed through my hands, creating a white glow in my palms. In my rage, I threw the two balls of glowing light at any or everything I could.

The glowing balls caught fire as they hit buildings and even people. I didn't care. My heart was broken. The only woman I had ever loved was now gone, and I couldn't even save her. I fumed at myself not even thinking about what I had done.

I didn't even question it. I had known I was different, so it didn't surprise me that I had some kind of power.

Then without warning, time stopped. Everyone was still in half run or mid-fall. I was the only one able to move freely or so I had thought. There was one other walking around, examining the carnage. He had long, black hair tied into a loose ponytail and pointed ears along with a pointed face. His eyes were a pale purple or lavender color. He had on a long, black coat and wore a top hat.

"Remy Christopher Jackson, come with me," he said, his voice low and musical.

# Chapter 22

*Aislin*

Everyone stood there, silence hanging like a fog thick in the air, after Remy told his tragic tale.

"Hold on a minute, that's how you found out you were a wizard just by shooting lightning or whatever out of your hands? Who is to say you aren't an elemental? It seems a little sketchy if you ask me," Kaydynce said, her blue eyes squinting.

"Well, that was just the start. I found out more while I was in that dark cell," he said, sheepishly.

He held out his hand, and a very old-styled book appeared out of thin air.

"This book appeared to me only moments after being taken. It's a book of spells. So naturally I figured out what I was since I couldn't be a witch. I was the male equivalent of a witch, a wizard."

Kaydynce continued to glare at him. I rolled my eyes then studied this so-called wizard. He had short, black hair and skin as dark as chocolate. He wore a white button up shirt with a tan vest over top and dark brown pants. His gold framed glasses barely hid his deep brown eyes. He had fine black hair above his lip. He didn't seem like a wizard, but I couldn't say anything since I'm a banshee and I don't quite look like one. Though Teagan was starting to.

"Well now that that is done and over with, I think it is time we leave before the court finds out what we have done," Ilium said, looking behind us.

I nodded about to take a step when I felt the first shake. It threw everyone off; some fell into the walls while others fell into each other. I stumbled backwards, catching myself. I studied Ilium, hoping my suspicion wasn't true. He stared back at me with fear in his indigo eyes.

"Please tell me it's not what I think it is," Teagan said, as another quake shook the walls and floor.

Cracks formed on the walls and ceiling as the quakes continued. Pieces of plaster fell from the ceiling, as the cracks grew wider. Ilium stared at us for one split second then yelled, "Run!"

As soon as the words left his mouth, he was gone. The quakes came one after the other along with the boom of heavy footsteps. I gulped, glancing toward the end of the hallway where the door was and watched as it shook.

"Aislin, come on!" Kaydynce yelled, tugging on my arm.

Everyone ran toward safety, pushing each other out of the way. I shook myself out of the trance and ran as fast as I could. We had just reached the door to the outside world when there was a crash. I glanced backwards and caught a glimpse of yellowish skin and legs as thick as redwood trees. My suspicions were confirmed. We were dealing with . . . a giant.

"Shit!" I shouted, running faster.

My hair whipped behind me as I ran, stumbling at each quake. We were outside at this point, but it didn't matter he was still after us. I stopped and turned around, facing the giant head on.

"Aislin, what are you doing?"

"We can't out run it, Teagan, there is only one way to get rid of him and that is to face him head on."

"Are you sure about this?" Kaydynce asked, as she stood beside me.

"There isn't another way."

"I will stand by you, Miss Aislin," I heard Remy say behind me.

I heard others follow suit. It surprised me, these people who had no clue who I was were lining up behind me without any complaint. I turned and looked at the group of supernatural beings that had joined forces with me to defeat the giant.

"I cannot guarantee any of you safety if we do this. Anyone can leave if they choose," I said, studying the different array of beings.

A few pixies, wolves, gnomes, and goblins scattered into the woods. I didn't blame them, hell I didn't want to be in this situation either. Instead of running, I had to suck it up and be a leader. The giant came bumbling through the doorway, smashing through it like it was nothing.

The doorframe busted and splintered as he barreled through it. His head stood a foot above the tree line when he stood up straight. He wore only a tan loincloth around his waist everything else was bare. His skin was the color of Gouda cheese, just a hint of yellow in white.

We stood there for a moment, staring at each other. It was a standoff and neither one of us was winning. He made the first move with a bellowing roar he charged. The ground shook with each stomp of his feet as they hit the grassy floor. "Get ready!" I yelled above the rising wind and roar of the giant.

The trees quaked and shivered in fear as the giant approached. I assumed a fighting stance though I knew I couldn't do anything. I didn't even have a weapon to defend myself. I wanted to kick myself for my foolishness. How the hell was I supposed to beat a giant without a weapon? I guess I was lucky I set free a bunch of supernatural beings with different powers, how convenient.

I pushed those thoughts away and tried to concentrate on the matter at hand, but then other thoughts popped up. I was momentarily distracted by thoughts of Kaelin when the giant slammed his fists into the ground, sending dirt and rubble flying in all directions.

Many were sent flying, caught off guard by its massive attack. I was thrown backwards, caught in the middle of the action. A cloud of dirt rose into the air as an elemental used his superspeed to disorient the giant. He must have been an air elemental with his wispy, white hair and smoke-like body. He would shift in and out of sight. While it was distracted a pixie threw pixie dust causing the giant to lift off the ground. The tiny creature's pale wings glistened in the light as the sun peaked through the clouds to watch the fight.

The giant became agitated and began thrashing in the air, sending gusts of wind in all directions. The elemental was thrown off balance as the gust hit him square in the chest. As the giant kicked and punched the air, the pixie got caught in one of those punches and went sailing. She hit a tree, landing awkwardly on one of her wings. I cringed, feeling sorry for the pitiful thing.

"Aislin, watch out!" I heard Teagan scream.

I peered back at the giant just in time to catch a glimpse of a fist hurtling toward me. I thought about running, but I knew that wouldn't do me any good. Maybe I could dodge and run up his arm like many video games I've seen. I would have tried, but of course I was too slow. His fist was just inches from me when I saw a flash of light. It was like a flash bomb had gone off, blinding everyone around it.

"Oops, sorry, wrong spell," Remy said, laughing nervously.

The giant roared, swinging his arms trying to swat at anything and everything he possibly could. Bodies went sailing through the air as his arms connected with beings in his path. One of those beings happened to be Kaydynce. I heard her yell in surprise along with many others. I looked behind me to find only a handful of supernatural beings left. *Well, I did say they could leave at any time, but I didn't think they would ditch during a fight.*

I shook my head and tried to concentrate on the fight at hand, which we were losing. There were only a few powerful supernatural beings standing behind me. Each one of them had wide eyes. Some were on the ground from being swept off their feet while others took fighting stances yet made no move to engage in it.

"We need to do something. Do something now, Remy!" I yelled.

I watched Remy flip through pages in some weird looking book, occasionally pushing up his glasses. He stood off to the side, away from the fight. I wanted to scream and rip out my hair. This was getting us nowhere. Somebody needed to take charge and enforce action. I wanted to point at someone passing the responsibility on, but I knew that was childish. I got us into this, which meant I had to finish it.

I studied my surroundings while dodging the giant's flailing arms and picked up a sturdy branch that had fallen from the onslaught of the giant's rage. I was ready to run and just stab it when I felt a light touch on my arm.

"Aislin, this is foolish. We cannot defeat this giant even with the help of these few people. We need to distract it and then run," Teagan said, grabbing my shoulder lightly but firmly.

"I just need to think of a plan," I said, while dodging flying rubble.

"I have an idea. My name is Aster," a small voice said from behind us.

I turned to find a girl barely pass the age of fourteen with long, black hair that was about as long as her whole body. She had dark grey eyes that told a story all their own. She wore a hot pink skirt and an AC/DC shirt. This was no ordinary girl. I figured she didn't appear her age either.

"If you can cause a distraction, Calumet and I can get him down on his knees for someone to take him out," she said, as her nails lengthened and formed claws.

I nodded while looking around to make sure nothing was coming our way. The girl motioned to a boy with spiky, blue hair and piercings all over his face. He had eyes that shifted from green to gold constantly. While his partner wore bright pink, he wore baggy, black pants with chains attached to them and a plain black T-shirt. While I was conversing with the two misfits, the giant had regained his sight and was storming toward us again.

"Remy, now!" I screamed, while getting into a fighting stance with my branch pointed toward it.

Time slowed once more, but this time I was moving in normal speed along with everyone else except the giant. The misfits took this opportunity to enact their plan. Both had superspeed though you could tell the difference of species. Calumet's hands had turned into hairy paws with sharp claws while Aster's hands remained the same except for her clawlike nails. One was a vampire while the other was a werewolf, an odd pair. The duo sliced through the giant's legs from behind the knee. The giant fell hard as time sped up again. His knees hit the ground, creating two craters along with seismic quakes.

My bones quivered; as the world shook around me then it was gone. Yet what wasn't gone was this giant who was trying to kick his legs, which weren't attached anymore. Blood spurted from his open wounds, pooling around him and soaking into the earth. I felt sorry for him at that moment. I knew I was doing him a favor as I ran and threw my branch like a javelin, piercing one of his eyes. His body flailed around yet he wasn't going down. I glanced over at Remy, pleading him with my eyes to put him out of his misery.

Remy nodded, frowning slightly as he flipped through the book again. As his flailing slowed, a bolt of lightning flew out of Remy's hand and hit the giant straight in the temple. He collapsed immediately, leaving behind a huge carcass. I let out the breath that I was holding and plopped onto the ground. I wasn't the only one relieved. Teagan and Kaydynce plopped down beside me, well Teagan kind of floated to the ground.

"I'm so glad that is over," I said, as I put my arms around their shoulders.

Kaydynce opened her mouth to say something but was interrupted.

"I see you have killed my pet. What a shame. I thought he would have eaten you by now," said a tinkling voice.

# Chapter 23



*Kaelin*

Darkness surrounded me once more, but unlike last time I was alone. I had given in to my fate. I knew there wasn't anything I could do. I just wished I could have had more time with her. It was like every time we found each other something tugged us apart again. Our lives had never been easy. I knew that and so did Aislin. Yet I had thought this time it would be different, that maybe we could finally be together. Fate had other ideas though.

I sighed, flopping down on the cold, dark floor or what I thought was a floor since I couldn't see a single thing. Darkness swirled around me, laughing and taunting. I knew it wasn't truly the dark. It was the part of my mind that stayed in the back, but every once in a while, would pop up whispering doubts and twisting my memories.

I brought my knees up and rested my elbows on them while resting my head in my hands. I hated myself for giving up so easily, but I didn't want anything to happen to her. I closed my eyes as memories flashed before them like a kaleidoscope. Images of Aislin laughing, frowning, flirting, and pure happiness on her face flinted across my mind.

I wanted to see her shining, blue eyes and run my hands through her mocha brown hair once more. I wanted to lean in close and inhale the scent of strawberries and candy. I wanted to feel her body pressed against mine, the soft touch of her lips as we kissed. There were so many things I wanted yet would never get the chance to do again. I balled up my hands into fists and pressed them against my forehead. At that moment I just wanted to punch something. I felt powerless. I couldn't do anything to save the love of my life instead I was left in the dark.

Time seemed to pass by slowly if there even was time in this place. If I stayed here much longer, I was afraid I would lose my mind. I couldn't stay here. I couldn't just sit here and wait for death, that wasn't like me. I was an action kind of man, which meant I was somehow going to find a way out, no matter what. I rose back up and paced around my prison cell, finding nothing but darkness.

I didn't want to give up yet how was I supposed to find a way out if I couldn't even see where I was going? I paced around the room, walking along beside the walls. I had hoped maybe there was a hidden door or something for me to sneak out of. There was no way out. Did I want to accept my fate? I couldn't, not if it meant I would never see Aislin's face again. I wasn't about to give up instead I planned and waited for my chance.

It didn't take long for me to put my plan into action. I waited in the dark, crouched down, ready to spring at anyone who came into view. Light soon spilled into the room as an invisible door opened revealing a short, stocky man with bright red hair. I barreled into him, pushing pass to freedom. I must have surprised him since he didn't chase after me. I shrugged, it made things easier. I ran down the hall, not recognizing anything. It was like I was in a completely different place. The walls were the same pale color, yet the floor had changed.

The floors were carpeted with a pale green color while the earlier floors were wooden. As I ran, I heard footsteps behind me. I wasn't surprised to find soldiers tramping after me. And when I say soldiers, I mean soldiers. They wore metal armor and helmets with red plumes. Their armor clanked as they ran. They even had spears pointed toward me. I probably should have been scared, hell anybody else would have, but I laughed at the situation. I'd rather go out like this than stuck in a cell or anything else. The wind brushed passed me as I maneuvered through the different halls.

What I hadn't predicted was a dead end, which I had finally come to. I was trapped. I turned around and faced my pursuers. I wasn't going to show fear or back down. I was going to face them head on even though I didn't have a chance of winning this fight.

"Come and get me!" I yelled, standing my ground.
"Finally, I found you." a voice said behind me.

I jumped in surprise about to say something when a hand touched my shoulder then darkness once more.

"Why does this keep on happening?" I growled just as lights appeared.

"You are safe now, Mr. Kaelin. I have brought you to my home until it is time for your friends to get you."

I backed up and stared at my new captor. He had white-blond hair that fell to his shoulders and purple eyes. I narrowed my own eyes. I recognized him from the court.

"Who are you and why am I here?"

"I am Ilium, and you are here for safekeeping as I have been asked to do."

"And who asked you to keep me safe?" I asked, suspiciously.

"I was asked by your friend, Kaydynce on behalf of your other friend, Aislin."

My eyes widened at the mention of Aislin. I smiled, thinking of how she always thought of others before herself.

She was so selfless.

"Okay, so I'm stuck here until someone comes to get me?"

"Yes," he said then cocked his head to the side, "I must go. My fair lady is calling me," he paused once more then grinned, "I will warn you though, there will be . . . temptations that are best to avoid."

"What kind of temptations?" I asked, but he was already gone.

I sighed. I guess there was nothing left but try to get comfortable. I checked out my surroundings and was surprised to find it quite nice. This Ilium guy had a nice pad. He had a 50-inch flat screen TV, a leather couch along with a matching love seat. The walls were a dark grey while the floors were a mahogany wood. He even had a kitchen, which was stocked full of every food imaginable. My mouth watered just at the sight of it.

As I admired the baby back ribs left on the counter, a door to one of the two rooms opened revealing a goddess. Her long silver hair fell pass her waist and covered her private parts and bright lavender eyes. I gulped.

"Fuck..."

# Chapter 24



*Aislin*

"My poor, poor pet. It grieves me to see him this way," the redhead from the court said.

She glanced at his body, but I didn't see a single expression of sadness cross her face. She didn't care if her "pet" was dead or not. A few stray hairs framed her face as her green eyes locked onto us. She stepped over a few pieces of rubble as she came closer.

"I see you have defeated him." She waved her hand in the air, frowning. "What a pity, I had hoped he would crush you all."

"Well, it seems you didn't have much hope in us," I said. My lips curved up into a smirk even though my insides were twisting and turning.

"I had hoped I had seen the last of both of you when I sent you to the abyss," she fumed, putting her hands on her slender hips.

"Well, **I** had hoped I had seen the last of you," Kaydynce shot back.

The redhead smiled, her fangs glistening in the light. Her eyes hardened.

"Ilium," she called, looking over her shoulder then back at Kaydynce with a smirk.

Ilium pushed through the crowd to the front to stand beside her. I heard Kaydynce gasp behind me. I was just as surprised as her to see him on the other side. As I stared at him, he winked, and I sighed in relief. He was on our side or at least I hoped he was.

"Ilium, kill them," she said, grinning at us.

My little group stood frozen as Ilium took a step toward us. He took a step then stopped, turning around to face the court's crowd. In a split second, the whole crowd collapsed as if all their legs just gave out. It was like watching a set of dominoes fall, one after the other. The redhead's mouth fell open.

I probably had the same expression on my face. I couldn't believe what had just happened. The redhead stood there, her face paling even more. Then in an instant her face turned a bright red as her nostrils flared and her eyes narrowed.

"How dare you disobey me!" she snarled.

Her fangs lengthened as she hissed. Her body had gone rigid. Ilium's indigo eyes seemed to gleam as a smirk appeared on his pale lips.

"I did not disobey, milady. I killed them for you," he said, bowing with his right over his chest.

"I meant them," she growled, pointing at my small little group.

"You should clarify who you want killed instead of disassociating yourself by using the word them," Ilium said, matter-of-factly.

I watched the scene unfold before me, blinking a few times to keep up. I couldn't believe he had disobeyed her, well, he was technically right since she hadn't exactly told him whom to kill. I was still stunned. The redhead was too and wasn't happy about it either. Her face had turned a purplish color as she sent daggers his way. Her glare could kill. I was so glad she wasn't a Gorgon or else we would have all been turned to stone.

As I watched the confrontation, I tried to think of a plan. I didn't know what the hell I was going to do to get out of this mess. I needed some kind of weapon, but where was I supposed to find one?

"Hey, Remy," I whispered, nudging him.

He jumped in surprise like he had been too absorbed in his book to pay attention to the world around himself. He peeked over at me, pushing up his glasses.

"Yes?"

"Is there any way you could conjure a weapon or something?" I asked, hoping he would say yes.

He held up one finger then sifted through his spell book. His brows furrowed as his eyes scanned the pages. I crossed my arms over my chest and tapped my foot. Ugh, this was taking too long.

"Did you find anything?" I asked, looking over his shoulder at his book.

I didn't know how he could read anything. It was all in some weird language with a bunch of symbols.

"Do you mind not hovering, ma'am, it's quite distracting."

I sighed, taking a step back so that I wasn't "hovering". I glanced back over at Ilium to see them still fighting. *Wow, way to go Ilium,* I thought to myself. He was rather good at causing a distraction.

"Aha," Remy said before chanting weird words.

When he finished, a sword materialized in his hand. It shone in the fading light. The hilt was adorned with rubies, sapphires, and emeralds like a king had owned it or something.

"Wow." I breathed as he handed it to me.

I had never wielded a sword before, and it was quite heavy. My right arm buckled a little as I took it. I didn't know if I could use it, but I was going to try. I gave it a test swing and almost chopped off Remy's arm.

"Sorry," I whispered, as I tried out my chopping moves.

I took a deep breath and started running toward the redhead with my sword behind me. I had to use two hands to hold it, yet I was still dragging it behind me. The tip was marring up the ground as I ran. I brought it up and swung at the redhead. She dodged it in a fluid motion. She laughed as her gaze fell on me.

"You're going to have to do better than that, missy.

I'm hard to kill."

Her green eyes gleamed as she crouched, hissing at me with her fangs extended. I tried another swing and missed again. I was either too slow or she was too damn fast. I tightened my grip on my sword and swung with all my might. She wasn't quick enough, and my sword grazed her neck. A thin line of crimson blood oozed from her neck.

"Lucky shot," she called, as she circled me.

I searched for someone who would help me out here. Remy was too busy reading his book, Teagan just floated there like nothing affected her, and Kaydynce just watched us like her favorite TV show was on.

While my eyes were scanning the crowd, I noticed the redhead out of the corner of my eye. She ran toward me with superspeed. I had just enough time to raise my sword before she pounced. Her body collided with mine. I shifted under her weight. A low slurp reverberated in my ears. I gasped. The hilt of the sword stabbed into my ribs. I-I did it...

"Um, a little help here, please," I said, struggling to move out from under the vampire's dead weight.

Ilium was the only one who came to my rescue. He rolled the court member off me. I couldn't believe how heavy she had become. I scrambled up and glared at my gang.

"Why didn't any of you help me?" I asked, crossing my arms over my chest.

Both Teagan and Remy ignored me. Remy was still too engrossed in his book while Teagan was lost in her own world. Kaydynce on the other hand was looking at me like I was stupid.

"Well, it's not like I could have stopped her," she said, picking at her nails.

"Um, hello, you can suck the soul out of people. Why didn't you?"

Kaydynce rolled her eyes. "Well, duh, vampires don't have souls. Everyone knows that."

I sighed, shaking my head. There was no point in arguing with her.

"Whatever, anyways, it's over thank God. Now can we go pick up Kaelin and go home?" I said, feeling like I was going to topple over.

Everyone nodded. Ilium created a door and opened it for us. Everyone ambled in except Ilium and me.

"Is she actually dead?" I asked.

Ilium shrugged, pushing me through the doorway into utter darkness.

# Chapter 25



*Kaelin*

"Fuck...," I said, trying to avert my gaze.

I shifted from foot to foot. It seemed I wasn't gazing down far enough as her long legs entered my vision. I couldn't help but stare at them. Her legs were an ivory color, which shone in the pale lamplight. As I stared at her legs, my gaze slowly drifted higher to her thighs. I heard a soft giggle and glanced up to find not one but two goddesses in the room. The new beauty was exactly like the other except their eyes and hair were switched. One had long silver hair and lavender eyes while the other had lavender hair and silver eyes. Either way, they were both naked.

*Well, shit.* This was going to be a problem.

"Are you our new plaything?" the lavender haired one asked, tilting her head to the side.

I gulped. I wasn't exactly sure what to do about this situation. As the lavender haired goddess tilted her head, her long hair moved with her, revealing a part of her breast. My body tensed up. This was not good, not good at all.

"What do you mean by plaything?" I asked nervously.

I wasn't sure if I wanted the answer.

"Something we can play with," the silver haired one said while the other said, "Humans are fun to play with."

Both women stared at me eagerly, like they were expecting me to do something. I backed up slowly.

"Um, I think you have mistaken me for someone else.

I am sure as hell not a plaything," I said.

*I wouldn't mind being their plaything though,* I thought then shook my head. I shouldn't be thinking like that. I wasn't that guy anymore. I had to remind myself that Aislin was going to pick me up and take me home. I closed my eyes and imagined her face: pale blue eyes, long dark brown hair, and a smile that lit up her face and eyes. I smiled as I imagined her here with me. Just as I was imagining her sauntering up to me and giving me a long kiss, I was shocked out of my daydream as I fell against the couch.

"Illy said he would bring us a plaything," the lavender haired one said, pouting her lush lips.

I pressed back against the couch, trying to get as far away as I could from the two. My heart thrashed against my chest. I needed to control myself. I searched around for an escape route. I needed to escape badly at this point. I was already feeling my resolve dwindle with each passing second as the women moved and more of their skin was revealed. I wanted to stay strong for Aislin, but temptation was staring back at me with two pairs of big eyes. I watched as they slowly crept toward me with smirks on their pale faces.

I found myself unable to move. I felt like a mouse frozen in fear, as a snake got ready to strike. This wasn't like me. I wasn't the scared one. Usually, I was the one who made the first move when it came down to stuff like this.

I was the dominant one. I was the man. Yet at that moment I felt like the virgin who hadn't experienced anything and thus had no clue what to do in this type of situation. I was far from that guy I had been before. If I wasn't that guy anymore then why did I feel like my heart was going to beat right out of my chest? This wasn't supposed to happen. I wasn't supposed to be tag teamed by two naked women. I was only supposed to be with one woman, and her name was Aislin.

I was about to push pass them when I felt a light touch on my shoulder. The next thing I knew I was sprawled out on the couch with two hungry vixens coming toward me. *How the hell did I get into this situation?* I asked myself, unable to find a reasonable answer. The lavender haired one bent over the side of the couch and started crawling toward me, her silver eyes sparkling with mischief. My breath hitched as I gazed at her.

*Shit, shit, shit.* I kept on repeating in my head until she stopped and straddled my lap. *Ah, hell!*

The other one knelt beside me with her head resting on my arm.

*Could this get any worse?* I asked myself.

Something thumped in the background. I craned my neck to look behind me to find a door had appeared. *Ah, FUCK.* The situation had just gotten worse as Aislin, Kaydynce, Teagan, Ilium, and an ebony-skinned guy walked through the doorway.

"What the hell!" Kaydynce said.

She was the first one to notice the two naked women and me.

"Um, it's not what it looks like," I said, trying to push myself into a sitting position.

"Oh, so you're not having a threesome on the couch?" she asked sarcastically.

"It's not like that. Aislin, please, do you think I'm enjoying this?" I said and then winced as her pale eyes narrowed.

"Ilium, take me home," Aislin said, turning away from me to stare at him.

He looked over at me, lips curving up and winked. "As you wish, Ms. Aislin."

Without moving a single muscle, a doorway appeared behind them. It shimmered, fading in and out of existence.

"Aislin, please," I said.

I scrambled up, pushing both naked women off me. My knees hit the ground first as I tried to stop her. I picked myself up and rushed to prevent her leaving, but I was too late. My outstretched hand brushed her fingertips as she disappeared into the darkness. Teagan and Kaydynce had already passed through. As soon as Aislin entered the entryway, it vanished. I ran my hand through my hair and clenched my jaw. Ilium continued to grin at me. I glared at him.

"Why the hell didn't you warn me, man?"

"I told you there would be temptations that would be best if you avoided."

"How the hell was I supposed to avoid that?" I yelled, motioning to the two naked women.

"Play?" one of them asked.

"You couldn't have been more specific? Wait, you know what just never mind."

Ugh, I couldn't believe what had just happened. How was I supposed to get out of this? It was like trying to calm down a raging bull or bear. I really didn't want to face the calamity that I had inadvertently caused yet I knew if I didn't then there would be a lot more damage to repair. I sighed, running my hand down my face. *God, I hope I can fix this. If not then I'm screwed,* I thought, sighing again.

"Ilium, can you take me to Aislin so I can patch up my stupidity."

"As much as your torture amuses me, I find I also want you to mend things with Ms. Aislin," he said.

He frowned, shook his head, and then opened the same doorway Aislin had gone through. I watched as it blinked in and out of existence as Ilium and I walked through.

# Chapter 26



*Aislin*

Tears streamed down my face like a waterfall the minute I stepped out into my bedroom. I couldn't believe he would do that to me. I had saved him, and that was how he was going to repay me? I wiped the waterworks away furiously.

"It will be okay, Aislin, he is just a stupid boy. You don't need him anyways," Kaydynce said, laying a hand lightly on my shoulder.

I glanced over at her and smiled weakly. "I'm fine,

Kaydynce, but thanks for worrying."

"Glad I could help," she said, smiling, "well, I should get going. There is no telling how long we spent in that hellhole. Grandma is likely fretting over my whereabouts."

I nodded and watched her leave my bedroom before I plopped down onto my bed and lay down.

"I too must leave."

I shot back up, completely forgetting that Teagan was in the room. I frowned as I stared at her flickering form.

"What do you mean you have to leave too?"

Her lips lifted into a smile yet her green eyes were cast down.

"It is time for me to move on," she said blatantly.

"I don't understand," I said.

My frown deepened as I realized all my friends were leaving me.

"I must go where all spirits go when they leave their bodies. I have done what was needed of me, so now I must depart. This will be the last time we will ever see each other. This will be my final farewell," she said as her ghostly form floated up to the ceiling.

"Teagan, wait," I called, jumping off my bed.

Her form paused for a moment.

"I cannot stay, Aislin, I must go. They are calling to me."

"I-I just wanted to say thank you for everything that you have done for me. G-Goodbye," I choked out, as my throat closed, and tears formed in the corners of my eyes.

"Goodbye, Aislin," she said, her voice barely above a whisper.

She smiled and then was gone. I closed my eyes as the tears streaked down my cheeks to land in little droplets on the floor. I fell back onto my bed and stared up at my popcorn ceiling. I just had a fight with the love of my life and now my best friend was gone. What else could happen? My heart was breaking into a thousand pieces. I was losing everyone I cared about in my life. I sighed, shuffling over to my pillow, and curled up, tucking my knees close to my chest. I held my pillow against me, crying into it.

There was a shuffling across my room. My head snapped up. I peeked up just in time to see Ilium and Kaelin walking through a now disappearing doorway. I sniffled as my nose began to run. Kaelin's golden eyes locked on to me like a laser locking onto a target. His eyes widened when he saw me. I guess I could only imagine what he was seeing. My eyes were probably bloodshot, the bags under my eyes were probably red and puffy, and my nose most likely had boogers and snot hanging down. The sight of me would scare a small child.

"Aislin, what's wrong?" He ran over to me, kneeling beside my bed. "Was it me? I'm so sorry if it was my fault, please don't cry."

I tried to smile. He looked so cute when he apologized. His brows furrowed, and his lips jutted out a bit. I felt like I should be comforting him even though I was the one crying.

"Ms. Aislin, this is not like you or at least not the Aislin I have met," Ilium said, frowning.

"I'll be fine," I said, wiping away the last of my tears.

"Aislin, I'm so sorry. I didn't mean to upset you in anyway. I guess I just didn't think about what I was saying."

I smiled, resting a hand on his cheek. His golden eyes glistened with unshed tears.

"I should be the one apologizing. I was the one who overreacted," I said.

"Mr. Kaelin was in the wrong, my dear Aislin, as he was the one fooling around with not just one but two elven women," Ilium said, a smile playing across his lips.

Kaelin jumped up and marched over to Ilium, grabbing him by the collar. "Hey. This is your fault."

Ilium continued to smile, his indigo eyes turning a shade of purple. I scrambled out of bed and pushed myself between them.

"Stop it, you two!" Aislin yelled.

"He started it. If he had warned me about his escorts, then we wouldn't be in this mess." Kaelin huffed. "Fine." He slowly let go of Ilium's collar.

Ilium continued to smile, his eyes gleaming with mischief.

Ugh, I knew I was going to have my hands full with these two.

"I did warn you, Mr. Kaelin, you must have not been paying attention."

Kaelin stiffened beside me. I rested a hand on his arm. He glanced down at me for a second then back to Ilium, his eyes narrowing into slits.

"Can you two get along just for a little while at least?" I asked, feeling exasperated.

They were acting like children, and I was getting tired of it. I put my hands on my hips and glared at them both. When I glanced over at Kaelin, he had his head down. Ilium on the other hand seemed content with a hint of glee in his purple eyes.

"I was merely saying Mr. Kaelin must not have heard me, but alas that is not why I have intruded on you, Miss Aislin. I came to inform you of our deal, which has not been paid in full. I will collect my favors when the time comes, but for now I must take my leave. Goodbye Miss Aislin, until we meet again." He bowed then disappeared.

"Well, that was interesting to say the least," I joked.

"Aislin, what deal was he talking about?" Kaelin said, with a frown on his face.

"Oh that, that's nothing. I just have to do a favor for Ilium is all," I said, brushing it off.

"What kind of favor?"

I shrugged, averting my gaze. I knew where this was heading, and I wasn't ready to get into another fight with him. I felt his hand touch my cheek and then lift my chin. I looked up into his honey eyes and saw the worry I had known would be there.

"Aislin, please, what kind of favor?" he said, searching my eyes.

"I don't know," I whispered, glancing down.

He lifted my chin again. "What do you mean you don't know?"

"Like I said, I don't know what kind of favor."

"Dammit, Aislin. You need to think before agreeing to things." He sighed, running his hands through his hair.

"I'm sorry, but it was the only way to save you."

Tears collected in the corner of my eyes, but not out of sadness. My hands balled into fists at my sides.

"There could have been another way," he said, shaking his head.

"Well, excuse me for wanting to get you out before the court killed you. Ilium saved you, and you should be grateful."

"Yeah, he may have saved me, but it was for a damn price," Kaelin growled.

"Ugh, I cannot do this right now, Kaelin," I said, throwing my arms into the air. "I'm sick and tired of fighting. All I want to do is sleep. You know what, I think it's best if you leave. I need time to process everything that has happened."

My body shook with a rage I hadn't felt before or maybe it was betrayal.

"I'm sorry." He bowed his head. "I-I'll leave you be then," he said, before walking out the door.

I stared at the door long after he had left, hoping he would come back, but he never did. I shuffled over to my bed and flopped down. I closed my eyes and drifted off into a fitful sleep.

# Chapter 27



*Kaydynce*

I staggered out of Aislin's house feeling like a horrible person. I had left my best friend to cry her eyes out over a stupid boy. I would have stayed, but I had other priorities to deal with like changing my clothes and making sure my grandma wasn't worried. She could handle some stupid boy problem anyways. She didn't need me. Hell, it was her own damn fault for getting herself into this mess.

I picked up my head and sauntered down the path. I wasn't going to let her problems ruin my day. I shook off the feeling of regret and walked straighter. She wasn't going to hold me back. I brushed a stray blond hair from my eyes and glanced around, confused. I was still in front of Aislin's house like I hadn't moved an inch. I frowned.

How was this possible? I could have sworn I was moving. I had felt the wind through my hair, but now the air was still like it was holding its breath. The air was electrified as the hairs on my arms stood on end. Everything around me was silent. The night had taken on a darker feel like something was going to pop out of nowhere and scare me.

My pulse sped up. The darkness caved in on me. My breathing became ragged. I was frozen to the spot. Then a doorway appeared before me. It was letting off a pale light, which made the darkness cower and creep away. My heart was still beating fast, but for a different reason this time. A smile crept up my lips as a figure slipped out of the doorway and into the light. His white hair glimmered in the light of the doorway like a beacon or halo. He glided over to me and took my hand. It was just as cold as it was when we met.

"It is time, my sweet," Ilium said.

I nodded. I felt like I was in a dream or trance of some kind. It felt surreal.

"Wait," I said, pausing, "where are we going?" He smiled. "We are going home."

I let go of his hand and crossed my arms.

"Where exactly is 'home'?" I asked.

"The other world. It doesn't have an actual name, but if you so choose you may give it a name, my love."
"All right, but I would have to see it first before I could name it," I said, as a smile played across my lips.

"As you wish, my dear," Ilium said.

His indigo eyes glistened in the light as he took my hand again and led me through the portal. I stopped once more.

"Wait, what about my clothes?" I asked.

My once perfect clothes were tattered and ripped from the trial and the abyss.
I felt Ilium's eyes scan down my body. "I shall get you new clothes, my love."

I nodded, smiling up at him as he led me through the doorway. All thoughts of my wellbeing and my grandma dissipated. The door closed behind us, engulfing us in darkness. I shivered.

The temperature had dropped a couple of degrees from the warm night air I had been exposed to. I tightened my grip on Ilium's hand, feeling his ice-cold hand against my now sweating one. It felt like eternity before another doorway appeared. I shielded my eyes as we wandered out into a bright light. As my eyes adjusted, I noticed a tall, white building with an elaborate French door.

"Wow." I breathed.

Ilium laughed beside me. He wrapped an arm around my shoulder and turned me the other way.

"This is what you should be wowing about, my dear," he whispered in my ear.

His breath tickled against my skin, sending shivers down my spine. I looked to where Ilium had turned me and gaped. I had thought the house was magnificent, but it was nothing compared to the view before me. It was like a scene from a painting. We were standing on a cliff overlooking a waterfall that flowed into the crystal blue water below. It was surrounded by greenery, colorful flowers of all sizes, and rolling hills that seemed like they would go on forever. The view was picturesque. I closed my eyes as a breeze tickled my skin, running through my hair.

"So, this is your world? Why would anyone want to leave it?" I asked, glancing back at him.

"Hunger, needs, not everything is given here. We do not have the same freedoms as humans do. We are all different, thus requiring certain needs that cannot be met here. For instance, it is forbidden to bring a human to our world yet there are some who need the essence of a human to survive. There are others who find this place horrendous and would rather live in the darkness of the human world." I nodded, that was understandable.

"Then there are the ones who hate the king and queen of our world and would rather be in the human world than try to overthrow them," Ilium said, looking down at me, "And that is where you come in, my sweet, for we will overthrow the kingdom. I shall be king and you, my dear, shall be my queen." I smiled. I liked the sound of that.

"Wait, how are we going to dethrone them by ourselves?" I asked, frowning.

Ilium smirked. "Well, it is quite simple, we will "persuade" some people to form a revolt," he said matter-of-factly.

"Oh," I said, as a grin spread across my face.

Ilium laughed. "Come, my love, we have a big day ahead of us tomorrow, and we must be well rested."

I nodded, letting him lead me through his French doors into his manicured home. It was just as beautiful inside as it was outside. The walls were painted alabaster white with a mixture of gold and red around the borders.

I took a deep breath and caught a whiff of lavender and cinnamon as I toured around the house. The kitchen was immaculate with its stainless steel appliances and marble countertops. My heels clicked against the mahogany wood floors as I paced. As my eyes roamed the area, I noticed there was only one bedroom off to the left, down a hall. The door was cracked open, allowing me only the slightest bit of a view of Ilium's bed.

I stared back at Ilium to find him grinning. I cocked my head to the side, stray hairs falling across my face. His eyes had taken on a darker hue, turning a dark purple.

"What?" I asked.

"It is nothing really, except you are a stunning specimen of a woman. I find myself staring at your beauty, wondering how one such as you could exist."

A soft giggle bubbled up as warmth spread up my cheeks. "I can't say I've ever been told that before."

"I am only stating what I find to be true," he said, brushing the hair behind my ear.

I closed my eyes, savoring the feel of his icy hand as it brushed my cheek.

"I doubt that. Aislin is prettier than me," I said, as resentment rose up in me.

Aislin had always been prettier than me. She had always had the attention of every guy, and she never knew it. All she could see was Kaelin and look where that got her. I didn't understand what was so special about Aislin. Yeah, sure she had the body of a swimsuit model, but I had the same figure, yet I could never get the stares she always got. I shook my head, scattering the thoughts, pushing them away.

"If Aislin were prettier than you, as you say, then I would have chosen her, yet I did not."

I stared up into Ilium's eyes and smiled slightly. I guess it had to be true, elves wouldn't lie or at least from what I read they didn't.

"Come now, let us get some rest," he said, ushering me into his room.

The room was dark as we entered it. I could just make out a bed and a nightstand beside it. With a snap of his fingers, the room erupted with light. The room was the color of brass. The bedframe was a light wood color along with the nightstand. The bedspread on the other hand was a rich mocha brown. Ilium tugged lightly on my arm, leading me to the bed. I sat on the edge of the bed and leaned back, sinking slowly into the mattress. The bed was so soft, like I was lying on a pile of feathers or cotton.

It shifted as Ilium lay beside me. I felt his arm wrap around my waist then I was lying on top of him. He shifted a little, fixing it so we were both on the bed the right way. I smiled, resting my head on his chest. I felt his chest rise and fall along with the beat of his heart. I closed my eyes, feeling the world drift away as sleep took over.

"Good night, my queen," Ilium whispered, right before I fell into blissful sleep.

# Chapter 28

*Aislin*

Waking up was one of the hardest things to do, especially after everything that had happened yesterday. I had to get up, though. School was calling my name. I sighed and sat up in my bed. I brushed the hair out of my face, sighing once more as I felt the rat's nest atop my head. It was going to be a pain to get that out.

It was one of the downsides to having long hair, hard to maintain. I pushed the covers off and got up. My body ached from the fighting and quite possibly all the tossing and turning I had done in the night. I wasn't the best sleeper in the world. Worrying about whether the rest of the court was going to come after me didn't help.

I strode over to my closet, feeling the cold seep into my feet. I didn't know what to wear, trivial I know, but I had to look good. I scrounged through the array of clothes, tossing them around. By the end of my searching, my room was a mess, like a tornado had blown through.

I picked up a plain blue V-neck shirt and a pair of black jeans, putting them on. I sauntered over to my dresser and picked up my brush. I tried running it through my knotted hair, but it was futile. I felt like I was trying to wrestle an alligator with the fight my hair was putting up. I huffed, deciding to put it up into a messy bun. I ambled out my room and down the stairs to the kitchen.

As soon as I reached the kitchen, I saw the dishevelment that was my mother. Her once glossy brown hair was matted and dull. She was stooped over the counter with her hands covering her face, but I knew she had been crying.

"Mom?" I said softly.

I wasn't sure how she would react. Her face lifted. Her blue eyes widened. There were streaks on her cheeks from her tears.

"Aislin, oh my God. I was so worried!" my mom exclaimed, jumping up and dragging me into a tight embrace.

Her whole body shook. I could feel her rapid heartbeat. I had never seen my mother like this. It was unnerving.

"I'm fine, mom," I said, as she let me go.

"What happened? The whole supernatural world is in an uproar, and I was told it was because of you," she said, her eyes searching for an answer.

I bit my lip. I had hoped my mom wouldn't hear, but fairies are gossipers. Of course she would know, nothing escaped her hearing.

"Well, um, you see they were going to kill Kaelin, and I tried to stop them. They threw Kaydynce and me into the Abyss. Long story short, I set everybody in the Abyss free and killed a court member, or at least I think I did."

"Aislin Briella Gray," she scolded, crossing her arms over her chest, "do you know what you have done?"

"I'm sorry. I just couldn't let them rot there. Some of them did nothing wrong, like Remy," I said, pleading with her to understand.

"The court will be searching for you and the ones you freed. This could mean war," she said, her voice quivering.

"I know. I just . . . I didn't know what else to do."

"I understand, sweetheart, I just hope the cost isn't too high. Some things can't be undone," she said.

Her blue eyes took on a faraway gaze. My thoughts went to Kaelin. I couldn't lose him, not after everything I had done to save him. My pulse quickened. I needed to warn him.

"I know," I said, kissing her cheek then bolted out the door.

I dashed into my car, hoping he was still at home. If the court really was after us, then we needed to stick together. I didn't know what I would do if he got hurt because of me. I sped off to his place. *Damn it.* I thought to myself, feeling anger and fear welling up inside of my body, leaving a sickening feeling in my stomach and chest. His truck was gone. I put it into park and leaned back. I clenched my jaw. If he wasn't at home, where could he be? My heart clenched. Did the court find him? Was he hurt somewhere? All those thoughts ran through my head. I needed to snap out of it. I was overreacting. I reached into my pocket and plucked out my cell phone. *I hope his number is the same,* I thought as I searched through my phone for his name. I hit the call button and held it to my ear. It rang for a bit.

"The number you have reached has been disconnected." "Damn it!" I yelled, throwing my phone.

I rested my head on my steering wheel, trying to control my anger. I needed to think rationally. If I weren't at home, where would I go? I banged my head on the wheel. I had been so stupid. The only other place he could be was school, which is where I should have been to begin with.

I sighed, turning my car back on and sped off to school. I hoped I was right. I pulled into the parking lot and bolted for the school. I pushed passed the bustling kids, as I searched around frantically. I scanned the crowd, looking for his golden eyes. I saw blues, greens, and browns yet I couldn't seem to find his unique golden ones. I was about to give up, thinking I had been wrong, when I caught sight of him.

"Kaelin!" I called out, running to him.

He stood at his locker, grabbing his books, when I tackled him. His books fell to the ground, flipping open and scattering his notes across the floor. We both ignored it as his arms wrapped around me. I shivered. His skin burned against my cold skin.

"Aislin," he whispered.

His breath tickled the nape of my neck. Heat sizzled up my body at the way he said my name. I buried my face into his chest, breathing in his woodsy scent.

"I'm sorry," I whispered.

Tears slowly fell, soaking his green shirt. His fingers brushed under my chin and lifted it until we were eye to eye. He smiled, his golden ones darkening. I closed mine as his hand caressed my cheek, wiping away my tears.

"It's not your fault. I would have been mad, too. I should be the one apologizing anyway."

I shook my head, sniffling. "I-I overreacted."

I cast my eyes down as shame colored my cheeks.

"You had every right to, Aislin," he said, lifting my chin again. I stared into his eyes, momentarily lost in the sea of gold. My breath hitched, I'd forgotten what I was going to say. He had that effect on me. It was like I was stupefied, unable to speak let alone breathe around him. He may be human, but he was supernatural to me. Sometimes I felt like the roles were reversed. I was the human, and he was the handsome, supernatural guy. I shook my head, getting rid of the fog that had clouded my mind.

"Would you like to get out of here?" he whispered in my ear.

My heart skipped a beat at his words as I felt the hair rise on the back of my neck. I shivered, his breath cool against my exposed skin. I gulped and nodded, unable to speak for a moment. A slow grin spread across his lips. My eyes trailed down to his perfectly sculpted lips. It was the slightest shade of pink, and my eyes couldn't stop staring. I wanted to kiss him so badly, yet I held myself back. I felt his eyes on me then. I met his gaze. His honey colored eyes had darkened, sending even more shivers down my spine. I took a shaky breath.

His hand captured mine and then we were gone, walking out of the school with such speed that I almost tripped over my own feet. As soon as we were out of sight, he turned, tugging me toward him. I fell against his chest. I could feel his lean muscles under my hands. I looked up at him.

His lips crashed down on mine. I was caught off guard for a moment. I relaxed into his body, becoming pliant. His lips were soft, which contrasted with the way he was kissing me. My hands travelled up his chest to wrap around his neck, pressing myself closer. His hands travelled up my sides to rest on my cheeks, cupping them like a fragile flower about to break. His hands were warm and soft against my face. I melted against him. Colors burst behind my eyelids: reds, blues, greens, and yellows.

Kaelin was the first to break away. His rapid breathing matched mine. I had forgotten to breathe. He rested his forehead against mine as our breaths mingled. His hands were still cupping my cheeks. I was on fire. It was as if flames were licking up my body. I stared into his golden eyes, which seemed to morph and shift as if a flame was flickering. "Aislin, I don't know if I've told you this, but . . . I love you."

My chest clenched as my pulse sped up. I couldn't remember if he had or not, but I felt like I was soaring just hearing him say those words.

"I love you, too," I said.

My cheeks burned. I averted my gaze, finally noticing where we were. We were still in the parking lot, and there happened to be someone watching. Red eyes stared back at me. It smiled, showing razor-sharp teeth. I shuddered.

"We need to leave. Now."

Kaelin nodded, leading me to his truck. A breeze kissed my hair, sending the scent of the woods toward me. I smiled;

remembering what had happened in the woods on my birthday then frowned as I remembered the red eyes and sharp teeth of the onlooker.

"Are you going to get in or not?" Kaelin asked, his voice light and playful.

I nodded, opening the door. Rust flakes dusted my shoulder. I brushed it off, getting into the truck. I shut the door behind me, more flakes falling.

"Sorry, she is an old beauty," Kaelin said, starting her up.

The truck rumbled to life, sputtering a bit.

"She's old all right, but I wouldn't call her a beauty," I said, laughing.

I glanced over at him, smiling, as he backed out of the parking lot. He smiled back then turned his attention to the road. As I studied him, I wondered how or why he had fallen for me, especially after what he had found out. The sky was a murky grey mixing with the dark clouds that seemed to collect, foretelling rain to come.

I bit my lip, wondering if rain would put a damper on where we were headed. I hoped it would keep others at bay. As I stared at the clouds, my thoughts turned to the two people I had lost even though I didn't really lose Kaydynce. I may not have lost her physically, but it felt like I had emotionally. Despite everything, I still considered Kaydynce as one of my best friends. Friends always had their ups and downs, right? I shook my head. I shouldn't be thinking about her. I had other things that needed to occupy my mind like where we were going or if we were being followed.

"You okay?"

I jumped a little, surprised by his voice. I looked over at him to find him staring at me.

"Yeah, I'm fine, just lost in thought."

"What kind of thoughts?"

"Oh, you know, the usual: life, the world, stuff like that." "Is that all?" he joked.

"Yup, so where are we going?" I asked, studying my surroundings.

"Well, you did say you were going to show me around, if I'm not mistaken," he said, grinning.

I smiled. It felt like ages since I had said that. I couldn't believe he had remembered. It was a distant memory. I had said it the day I had my first Death Call.

"Earth to Aislin, you all right over there?"

I shook myself out of it and looked back at him. He had a frown marring his lips. His golden eyes bore into mine.

"Yeah, why?"

"I don't know you just seem sad all of a sudden."

"Oh," I said, glancing down at my hands.

I should have known he'd notice how I was feeling.

"Are you going to tell me what's wrong or am I going to have to pry it out of you?"

I sighed. "It just seems like I said that a long time ago." I paused, taking a deep breath. "Also, that was the day I saw how you would die, my first Death Call."

"Oh, is that all?" he tried to joke, but I could hear the undertone of worry.

"Kaelin, I don't want to lose you."

We stopped suddenly. Were we finally there? He turned to face me, reaching out a hand to grab mine. I took it, holding on tightly. I gulped as I stared up into his eyes. There was a moment of complete silence. It was like the world had stopped just for a moment. My pulse raced as I waited for him to say something.

"You won't, I promise," he whispered, giving my hand a light squeeze.

I smiled, hoping he was right as he opened the door and got out. I followed him, stumbling a bit. He caught me and jerked me into a hug, swinging me around. I couldn't help but laugh. My heart was light as he put me down. I clung to his arm as I tried to steady myself. He held onto me as we strolled to his house.

"My Dad is out with his girlfriend, so we have the place all to ourselves."

My cheeks heated up at the thought of being completely alone with Kaelin. In his house. Kaelin laughed beside me. It sounded like rolling thunder as it sent chills down my spine.

"Don't look so nervous, Aislin," he chuckled.

"I'm not nervous." I retorted a little too loudly.

My pulse was racing as we reached his door. He stopped. I peeked at him curiously then squeaked in surprise as he pushed me up against the door. My heart thrashed against my chest as his body pressed against mine. I took in a shaky breath.

"Kaelin," I whispered, right before his lips found mine.

My eyelids slid down as the pressure of his body against mine and the warmth of his lips engulfed me. I could feel his heart racing or was that mine? I was the first to break the kiss, leaning my head against the door. My breathing was even more ragged than before as I tried to catch my breath.

Kaelin smirked, his eyes shining like liquid gold.

"Your cheeks are flushed," he whispered in my ear.

I shivered as his cool breath tickled my skin.

"And yours aren't?" I said, out of breath.

"I have more control," he whispered, as he kissed my neck.

Goose bumps surfaced on my skin, sending chills down my spine. My pulse spiked as his lips touched my exposed neck. I could feel his lips spread up as he smiled. He took a step back, putting enough space between us that I couldn't feel his warmth anymore. My legs went out from under me as I slid down the door. His laughter reverberated through my body. The sky rumbled to life.

"What's wrong, Linny?" he said, grinning.

I glared up at him. He knew exactly what was wrong, and he was enjoying it.

"Jerk," I mumbled, trying to get my bearings again.

He held out a hand. I took it graciously though I was mad at myself for the way my body had reacted. Nothing was worse than feeling helpless, like a deer caught in headlights. A streak of lightning rippled through the clouds. The sky opened, releasing the rain. It pelted our clothes. Kaelin helped me up, shielding my body from the rain, and unlocked the door. He pushed it open, shuffling us inside.

"Welcome to my humble abode," he said, his voice dripping with sarcasm.

I rolled my eyes and looked around. The place was spotless except for a piece of paper on the floor. I bent down and picked it up.

*Dear Kaelin,*

*Rebekah and I have left for the weekend. There is food in the refrigerator and pantry if you get hungry. Remember to clean up after yourself if you have any friends over. Don't forget to do the laundry.*

*Love, Dad*

"Hmm, does he write letters like this often?" I asked, turning to stare at Kaelin.

He nodded, not looking at me. I frowned, studying him.

"Hey, is everything all right?" I asked, resting a hand on his shoulder.

"Yeah."
"Kaelin, what's wrong?"

"Nothing, just forget about it," he said, shuffling toward the kitchen, "you hungry?"

I sighed, knowing he wasn't going to tell me. He had the ability to hold everything inside, bottling it up until he exploded. I sauntered over to the lime green counter and leaned against it as Kaelin rummaged through the refrigerator. "Find anything good?"

"We have cheese, jalapenos, mayo, mustard, milk, and grapes . . ."

"That's an interesting combination of foods," I said, grimacing.

Kaelin closed the fridge and opened the freezer. The cold spilled out like wisps of smoke. He sighed, shaking his head. "All that's in here are TV dinners and frozen vegetables."

"What kind of TV dinners?" I asked, pushing away from the counter and went over to him.

"The crappy kind that barely fills you up," he said, turning toward me. "You want to call in take out?"

I shrugged. Why not, it's better than TV dinners. Kaelin grinned, closing the freezer door. His golden eyes lit up as we stared at each other. I smiled, getting lost in his eyes. I broke away, glancing down at my ballet flats. My body warmed as a blush spread up my cheeks. I didn't understand why he was having this much effect on me. I took a deep breath, inhaling the scent of sweat and the woods in autumn, his scent. I could feel the heat radiating off him as his hand cupped my cheek.

"Aislin . . ." he whispered, his voice husky.

I looked up as I leaned into his palm. His hand burned against my cheek, but I didn't care. "Yes?" I whispered, captivated.

"You want pizza?" He smirked.
His golden eyes danced as I scolded.
"Jerk."
"You love it," he said.

His hand slid down my cheek, leaving a trail of heat, as he took a step back. He picked up his home phone and dialed the number for pizza. An hour later we were sitting on his leather couch eating pepperoni pizza. The air was thick with silence as we both ate. I wasn't sure what to say as we sat beside each other, barely touching.

Rain pounded the windows and roof. I bit my lip trying to think of something. After everything we had been through you would have thought I'd have something to say instead of sitting there like an idiot. I should have been worried about The Court finding us not about something interesting to say.

I sighed, hanging my head.
"So . . .?"
"So what?" he asked.

I glanced at him to find him grinning like the Cheshire cat. I shook my head.

"I was trying to get you to talk since we have been sitting in utter silence for the past thirty minutes."

"Maybe I don't want to talk," he whispered.

Chills went down my spine at his words. If he didn't want to talk then what did he want to do? My thoughts travelled to other places. My breath caught in my throat. Warmth radiated off him. My heart hammered against my chest. He was mere inches from me now. I stared into his honey eyes, mesmerized. I was paralyzed, heart fluttering. His lips grazed mine, starting a fire through my body. My arms latched around his neck, bringing him in closer. Kaelin lowered me down onto the couch, our bodies melding together. His hands found their way into my hair as he deepened the kiss. His heart raced, matching mine.

"Kaelin," I whispered against his lips.
"Yes?" His voice huskier than usual.

"I-I want to . . ." I gulped and opened my eyes. Heat coursed through me as I thought of a way to say it. "I want to give you everything: my heart, body, and soul."

His eyes widened and darkened at the same time, making me shiver. My breath hitched at the intensity in his gaze.

"You sure?" he whispered, as his eyes searched mine.
I stared back. "I've never been surer in my life."

I didn't have to tell him twice as his lips crashed against mine again, wilder than before. His hands skimmed down my body, leaving a trail of heat behind as he pressed against me. I clung to him, our breaths mingling as we came up for air. My fingers tangled in his red-brown hair as his lips left mine and travelled down. His kisses were feather light as his lips grazed my skin.

"Kaelin," I whined, squirming under him.

He laughed, kissing me lightly as he lifted me up. My body shook against him. He lifted me in one fluid motion. My legs automatically wrapped around his waist the minute he stood. His hands clasped around my rump.

"To my room then," he whispered in my ear.

# Chapter 29

*Kaelin walked aimlessly, like he was in a trance, toward the woman in black. The street was empty, not a car in sight. The darkness seemed to swallow up the glow from the streetlights only allowing a sliver of light to illuminate the scene. The woman's long wavy, red hair cascaded down her back. Her face was covered by her bangs yet her glowing green eyes could still be seen. Her black dress clung to her body like a second skin, accentuating her curvaceous figure.*

*"Kaelin O'Neil," she purred, her red lips curving up into a smile.*

*His body jerked to a stop in front of her. He was scarcely wearing anything, only pajama bottoms. His toned chest was bare, showing off his six-pack. The woman took a step closer to him, running a red fingernail down his chest, leaving a trail of blood.*

*"Such a waste," she whispered, leaning in closer and licking the blood away, "no matter, it must be done."*

*Kaelin's body trembled. Her lips lifted, revealing pointed fangs. She straightened and looked into his eyes.*

*"I release you," she said, her tinkling voice hypnotic.*

*Kaelin stumbled backwards.*
*"What the hell?" he exclaimed.*
*The woman smirked. "Now the fun begins."*

*She lunged at him with blinding speed. Kaelin didn't even have a chance to run as her fangs sank into his exposed neck. He struggled, trying to push her off, but it was futile. The more blood she drank, the weaker he became until she finally let him go. He crumbled to the ground like a puppet with its strings cut.*

I sat up, gasping for air. My heart thrashed against my chest. Sweat dripped down. My throat was sore and scratchy. My hand instinctively went to the other side of the bed, searching.

"Kaelin?" I whispered, my voice hoarse.

Silence greeted me. Panic started to settle in as I threw off the covers and put on my clothes. My hands shook as I stumbled around the room, calling his name. The house was quiet except for the echoes of my calls. I choked on a sob as realization sunk in. They had found him, or at least one member had. I cursed Ilium as I ran through the house, hoping I was wrong. I wouldn't let it happen. I was going to save him. I had to. I wasn't going to let him be killed by one of the Court. I saved him from their clutches once, and I could do it again.

My bare feet pounded on the wood floor as I dashed out of the house and into the street. The sky was pitch black, not a star in sight. I shivered, the hair on the back of my neck rising. I didn't stop running. I couldn't, not until I had found him. How had this happened? I couldn't fathom why this was still happening. I wasn't going to lose him, not again.

"Kaelin!" I screamed, as they came into sight.

The red haired woman towered over him. Her hair fell across his shoulder like a stream of blood. I froze. His golden eyes found mine. He mouthed something, but I was too far away to read them clearly. He might have mouthed, *"I'm sorry,"* before the light went out of his eyes and crumbled to the ground. The strings had been cut. His life had been snuffed out in a matter of seconds. I hadn't been fast enough. No—he can't be—oh God no. Pain ripped through my chest. I stumbled forward.

"No!" I screamed, tears streaming down my cheeks.

Anger and sadness bubbled up inside, ready to explode. I couldn't lose him, not now—-not after everything.

"Damn you!" I yelled, my fist shooting out toward the woman.

She laughed, dodging it effortlessly.

"You're going to have to do better than that, Aislin Gray."

I growled, striking at her again. She dodged my punch, but I was ready for that as I kicked out her legs. She flipped backwards, smirking. She spread out her legs, lowering her body into a fighting stance. She beckoned me forward with her hand. I narrowed my eyes yet ran toward her again. Her eyes glowed as she waited for my punch. I wasn't going to fall for it. Instead, I flipped over the top of her and kicked her in the back, landing on my side. My arm burned from the fall as I picked myself up quickly, ignoring the pain. I spun back around to face her, but I wasn't quick enough. Her hand latched on to my neck, lifting me off the ground.

"This has been fun, but I think it is time I ended it for good," she said, withdrawing an intricate stick from her cleavage.

The stick morphed into a broad sword that pulsed red with magical energy. The blade wasn't made of any sort of metal, as it was transparent except for the red glow. The handle had an elaborate leaf design while the energy blade was curved and jagged. I struggled, scratching at her hand with my nails. I gasped for air, kicking my feet. My mouth opened and closed with no oxygen going through. I was a fish out of water.

"Your death shall be slow and painful, by me, Seraphine," she whispered in my ear, as she thrust the sword through my stomach.

I didn't feel the pain at first just heard the slurp and tear as it entered my body. She released my throat and started to leave. I collapsed to the ground, blood seeping through my clothes and pooling around me. My hands grabbed the sword, yanking it out. I gasped as it slipped back out with a sucking noise. I looked down at the red puddle that was slowly spreading. My hand automatically went to my wound, trying to cover it up. I tried to stand. I stumbled up, wobbly from the lack of blood. There was no pain or if there was, I was numb to it.

I gripped the sword tightly in my hand, feeling anger and grief manifest itself. The sword changed suddenly. The handle lengthened until it was as long as I was tall and on either end was a curved blade that glowed white. I watched the retreating form of Seraphine and clenched my jaw. I clutched my stomach and ran at her. Just as she was turning, I swung my blade. She dodged, but I was ready and came back around with the other end. Blood spewed everywhere as her head fell and rolled away. Seraphine's body fell to the street.

I stumbled back over to Kaelin and fell to my knees. I collected his body into my arms and held him, weeping. His body had grown cold. A sob was wrenched from my throat.

"Damn it, Kaelin, you said I wouldn't lose you," I whispered, tears streaking down my cheeks to land on his pale skin—skin that would never feel the touch of my hand again. Blood pooled around us, a dark blob on an unlit street.

*Maybe we would be together in the afterlife*, I thought as the world around me darkened. My vision blurred then ceased.

# Epilogue

"She has suffered a major injury. If he hadn't found her, she would have surely been dead."

Someone in the background started weeping, but that couldn't be right. My eyelids fluttered open, trying to focus on the people surrounding me. My mom was seated beside me holding my hand as a stray tear fell softly on top of her hand. My grandma was there too though her dark blue eyes were bare as she stared down at me, shaking her head.

I didn't understand as the doctor's voice finally registered. Someone had saved me, but whom? My eyes scanned the room until they landed on a pair of dark brown ones. I smiled weakly. I hadn't seen him since the whole court thing. Remy had saved me.

"Kaelin?" I whispered, hoping maybe it had all been a dream.

Remy averted his eyes, unable to keep my gaze. I looked over at my mother, wincing slightly as I turned my head.

"I'm sorry, sweetheart, he's gone," she said, patting my hand.

I snatched my hand away, shaking my head. No, it couldn't be true. He couldn't be gone.

"No," I said, my voice hoarse.

"Calm down, everything is going to be okay," she said, reaching for my hand again.

How can you even say that? Kaelin is dead because—because I didn't make it in time. How can I ever forgive myself?" I said, my voice rising.

"Time heals all wounds," my grandma said coolly.

I glared at her. For once in my life, I hated her. I hated her cool demeanor, I hated her attitude toward everything, and I hated her for not being the caring grandma I used to know.

"Get out," I whispered, then said it even louder, "**Get out!**"

My grandma stared me down for a moment, not saying a word then left. My heart pounded against my chest. The monitors around me beeped frantically. My mother stared at me with wide eyes. I closed my own, taking deep, calming breaths.

"She means well," she whispered, her voice shaking.

"I-I can't handle that. Not right now. I-I need space." I sighed.

She nodded in understanding then stood up, giving me one last glance before she shuffled out the door. Remy was the only one left in the room. The doctor must have snuck out while I wasn't paying attention. Remy's eyes were still downcast.

"I'm not giving up," I told him.

He glanced up. His face scrunched and his brows furrowed. "Not giving up on what?" he asked, his voice going up an octave.

"I am **not** giving up on him. He is not completely gone. He can't be."

I knew in my heart that he wasn't gone. I just needed to prove that my heart was right.

"Aislin, you're speaking nonsense," he said, frowning.

"We can bring him back, Remy. We just have to find his soul."

"Aislin, what you are talking about is forbidden."

"I don't care. I'm not going to lose him!" I yelled.

Remy sighed, running a hand over his shaved head.

"Very well, if we are going to bring him back, we need to prepare. It may take some time."

"Okay, how long?" I asked.

"A year."

"A year!" I exclaimed, my hands clenching the bed sheet.

Remy scolded, pushing up his glasses.

"It's either a year or not at all. The magic you want me to use is very complicated and involves a lot of training. You will also have to train if you want to get his soul back."

I sighed, nodding. I would do anything to get him back, even if that meant sacrificing myself.